THE EMPTY FRAME

Magnus slipped through the door and made his way down the stone spiral stairs. Each landing was lit by a small spotlight, but in between the floors there was a deep darkness. His heart bumped as he picked his way down the smooth cold treads, his ears strained for the sound of the weeping voice. He could still hear it, though it was very faint now, and it seemed to come and go as if the troubled woman was wandering about, all over this rambling place, coming near to him and then withdrawing when she did not find what she sought.

THE EMPTY FRAME

Ann Pilling

An imprint of HarperCollinsPublishers

Also by Ann Pilling

Amber's Secret
Black Harvest
The Pit
The Witch of Lagg
The Beggar's Curse

First published in Great Britain by Collins in 1997
First published in paperback by Collins in 1998
Collins is an imprint of HarperCollins*Publishers* Ltd,
77-85 Fulham Palace Road, Hammersmith,
London W6 8JB

The HarperCollins website address is
www.**fire**and**water**.com

3 5 7 9 11 10 8 6 4 2

Text copyright © Ann Pilling 1997
Cover illustration by David Wyatt

The author asserts the moral right to be
identified as the author of the work.

Printed and bound in Great Britain by
Omnia Books Limited, Glasgow

ISBN 0 00 675293 4

for Joe, with love always

There is no fear in love; but perfect
love casteth out fear: because fear
hath torment.

1 John 4, 18

"The Admiral relates how he was sitting up late one night with his brother, over a game of chess, in a panelled room overlooked by the portrait of Lady Hoby. "We had finished playing, and my brother had gone up to bed. I stood for some time with my back to the wall, turning over the day in my mind. Minutes passed. I suddenly realised the presence of someone standing behind me. I tore round. It was Dame Hoby. The frame on the wall was empty. Terrified, I fled the room."

from *The Story of Bisham Abbey*
by Piers Compton

I

Floss was fed up. She was looking at herself in the mirror and she didn't like what she saw, neither her mop of dark hair, so frizzy and so coarse ('pan-scrubbers' a boy had said once) nor her stupid little nose, nor the fact that she was too short to be an actress and seemed to be putting on weight. She didn't even like her name.

Floss was short for Flossie, and both were short for Florence. She hated all her names this morning, she wanted something dignified and mysterious, a name like Hepzibah or Beatrice, something with history behind it.

'Sam, what do you think Lady Macbeth's name was?' she asked her brother, who was sprawled across the floor looking at a map. He too was stocky and short and he too had pan-scrubber hair, though it didn't seem to bother him.

"Dunno. Mavis I should think.'

Floss threw her book at him. It was Mum's *Complete Shakespeare*, it was big.

'Ouch! For heaven's sake, Floss.'

'Sorry.' She rescued the book, relieved to find

that it was still in one piece. 'It's just that I'm so depressed. I'll never get this part. My hair's not right and I'm too short. They'll give it to Anna Houghton. She's tall and she's got the most brilliant hair.'

'Looks aren't everything,' Sam said. 'Anna Houghton's dim, anyhow. I bet she doesn't understand what the play's about. Which bit are you doing, anyway?'

'The sleepwalking scene, where she comes on wringing her hands, when she can't get rid of the guilt about them having murdered the old king. It's funny, when they actually kill him she's the strong one. Macbeth behaves like a real wimp. But when things start catching up with them she's the one that goes mad.'

'And what happens?'

'She kills herself – but not on the stage.'

'Glad about that,' Sam said. 'I don't fancy watching you do that to yourself. Go for it anyhow, that's what Mum and Dad said. I bet you'll get it.'

Floss curled up again in her chair and tried to get the lines into her head. Their year was putting on *Scenes from Shakespeare* for the school's Christmas drama competition, and she wanted to be Lady Macbeth. She had planned to get the part word-perfect by the end of the summer holiday, but now they were going away and she wasn't sure she'd be able to learn all the lines. Perhaps she'd relax, instead of swotting up Shakespeare. The audition might be too nerve-racking. Anyhow, there was Magnus. Mum and Dad had said they must look after him.

'Do you think it'll be all right, going away with Magnus?' she asked Sam. At first he didn't answer, merely crouched lower over his map. Magnus, the boy their parents were fostering and who now lived with them, was a subject they found it difficult to discuss. They both had strong feelings about him.

'It's on a river,' he said, 'quite a big one. It looks like a tributary of the Thames. There'll be boats I should think. It'll be great if this hot weather keeps up. There's a swimming pool too.'

'But what about Magnus? I don't think he can swim.'

'He'll be fine. We can teach him,' Sam said easily. He was the unflappable type, a good foil for Floss who tended to panic.

'What do you really feel about Magnus living here?' Floss asked him, shutting the book. She was definitely abandoning Shakespeare for the day.

Sam folded his map up, very precisely and slowly. Then he took in a deep breath and let it out, also very slowly. 'I'm not sure,' he said. 'It's not that I don't like him. I mean there's nothing to dislike, is there? He hardly ever speaks.'

'No, but when he does it's something he's really thought about. Have you noticed? I think he's rather clever.' The truth was that Floss thought Magnus quite amazingly clever. When he came out with his quick, precise observations she felt like a dinosaur plodding around in gum boots.

'Well of course he's clever,' Sam said. 'But then, his father was some kind of genius wasn't he, in a university?'

'I think so. I wish we knew a bit more, though. I mean, I know it's awful, how he's been treated, but we've got to live with him.'

'Well, I'm not sure I'd go round telling people about my mother going to pieces, when my father had just walked out without a word, and had never come back. They sound *weird*. That's when his mother started doing strange things, and ill-treating him, according to Dad.'

'But why did nobody *know*?'

'Well, I think she, sort of, withdrew from everybody, with Magnus. She actually went to live in another town, where no one knew her. His father had been teaching him at home, so his school wouldn't have missed him and I suppose outsiders didn't want to barge in. I mean, they must have been very respectable, not the kind of people social workers are asked to investigate, unless someone tells them to.'

'And nobody did?'

'No, not until it was too late, not according to Mum and Dad.'

'I wonder why the father walked out?'

'Dunno, but I don't think he went off with someone else. Dad said he'd got very stressed-out, about his work, he said it was all that mattered to him. He was obviously an unbalanced kind of person. That's why he pushed Magnus so hard, at his lessons. I should think it's why he won't always co-operate now, at school. He's digging his heels in. Don't blame him either.'

'He's getting a lot better though.'

'Yes, I know.'

'But why didn't the mother protect Magnus more? That's what mothers do.'

'Perhaps she was frightened of the father. She can't have been very tough, she's had some kind of mega mental breakdown now, that's why he can't go to see her.'

'Poor old Mags. You do mind him being here though, don't you, Sam? Why?'

Sam sat back on his heels. 'I don't know,' he said. 'I didn't think it would matter so much. I know Dad and Mum care about us just the same but it feels different now, that's all. It's how I feel. I can't help it.'

Floss said, 'But Sam, he cries in the night, he really sobs. It's awful.'

'I know.'

'The fostering person told Mum and Dad he'd been beaten, and shut in cupboards, things like that. And when she was ill his mother made him do all the housework. He was only little, it went on for ages. How *could* she?'

'I've told you, because she was sick, in her mind. They don't keep people in hospital for nothing. They must think Magnus is better off with us, for now.'

Silence fell in the shabby, familiar sitting room. Privately, both sister and brother had minded the coming of Magnus, an eleven-year old boy to whom these terrible things had happened, but they'd promised their parents that they'd try to make him feel welcome. And they were trying. It was hard though, with somebody so unresponsive.

'He won't be with us for ever,' Floss said firmly.

'No.' But Sam didn't sound very convinced. His parents had big hearts. He suspected they would hold on to Magnus, if it was humanly possible.

'Well, this holiday might help,' Floss said, perking up. She had more or less decided not to audition for Lady Macbeth and at once she felt a lot more cheerful. 'Tell me where we're going, again.'

'Why don't you look it up for yourself?' Sam said, putting his map inside a folder labelled ABBEY in neat, square printing.

'I've not had time, with the play and everything. Come on.'

'Well, I've told you, it's on a river.' Sam said. 'Mum's cousin sent that booklet about it, you could have read it.' But actually he quite liked telling Floss things. She was cleverer than he was, though not in the same league as Magnus. 'It started as a kind of religious house, for pilgrims travelling to shrines. They used to stay there on the way.'

'Sort of – mediaeval bed and breakfast?'

'Yes. But they said prayers for you.'

'Then what happened to it?'

'Well, according to the book some monks took over, Henry the Eighth chucked them out in the end. He seems to have got quite fond of the place himself. He could sail down to it from London, on the river. Queen Elizabeth slept there too.'

Floss snorted. 'Come off it. Surely you don't believe *that*.'

'Why not? She slept everywhere.'

'Well, that's what I mean. So how did Mum's relation come to own it?'

'I'm not sure she does own it, not the whole place. There's a man called Stickley. He's related to her and he's the one that seems to run it. I think it was left to them both in a will.'

'*Stickley*…' Floss mused. 'It sounds horrible. So why did they turn it into a sports centre? It must have been gorgeous once, from that picture Mum showed us.'

'They needed money to keep it going, I suppose. At least they still live in it. Anyhow, we'll have the run of the whole place, with luck. There's a swimming pool, and tennis courts, and all those keep-fit machines.'

'Ugh,' said Floss.

'It might get your weight down,' Sam said slyly. 'I don't suppose Lady Macbeth went to Weight Watchers. All that wringing of hands – she was probably anorexic.'

Floss picked up the Shakespeare. This time she really *would* throw it at him. But then she put it down again hurriedly. Someone had crept into the room, switched on the television and was sitting in front of it, perched very neatly on a bean bag.

'Hi, Mags,' she said to the small humped figure. 'Are you all packed up? The taxi'll be here soon.'

'Yes.'

'Put in your swimming things?' Sam said. 'There's a pool and there won't be anyone else there, with luck.'

Magnus didn't reply but stared at the television screen on which some politicians were arguing about the dumping of nuclear waste. He was odd. He often watched the most boring programmes but if you looked closely you could see that he wasn't watching at all but staring beyond the screen, thinking his own private thoughts.

'Come and talk to us, Mags,' Floss said gently, switching off the TV and joining him on the bean bag. As she squished down, some white pellets seeped out of a hole. Magnus picked them up and put them carefully on the mantelpiece. 'It needs mending,' he said, 'or it'll get worse. I could sew it up, while your mother's away.'

'Yes, but listen, you don't have to. She doesn't expect you to do things like that.'

Magnus liked doing little chores but their mother tried to discourage him. His own mother had made him do the housework. Theirs wanted him to have some childhood, before it was too late.

He was nearly twelve now, two years younger than Floss and three years younger than Sam. He was short too, like them, but very thin and bony. Now and again Floss tried giving him little hugs but he didn't seem to like them, and besides, it was like putting your arms round the frail and delicate skeleton of a tiny bird. You felt he might crack. He had fine pale hair, an ashy gold, and deep brown eyes.

'Lovely colouring,' Mum said, the night he arrived. 'He'll break a few hearts, he's going to be absolutely gorgeous.' And Floss, fighting with unexpected jealousy, had said 'Yes'. (Nobody had ever said *she* was gorgeous.) But Magnus had turned away his face.

The journey to the Abbey took much longer than they had expected because they had to go on three separate trains, zig-zagging down the country. They were on their own, with Sam in charge, and they had their instructions. If anything went wrong, or they got separated, they had to phone Cousin M at the Abbey, or the airport hotel where their parents were staying. They flew out next morning to a flat in Majorca which Cousin M was lending them for a holiday. Magnus could have gone with them, he was very attached to Mum. But he'd decided to go off with Sam and Floss instead, which had pleased everybody because the main purpose of Mum and Dad's going away had been to leave the three children to get to know each other.

It was nearly dark when a taxi drove them into the Abbey grounds. Magnus had fallen asleep and the others were trying hard not to. They were keen to see everything but it had been a very long day and they were even more keen to drop into a comfortable bed. As the taxi crunched up a long gravelled drive towards a dark hump of buildings, an owl hooted and bats swooped down towards the windscreen, then away. Sam felt excited. 'It's like a film set,' he said, 'it's brilliant!'

'Mm.' Floss muttered. She wasn't sure. It seemed a bit spooky to her. And why had Mum's cousin sent a taxi for them, instead of coming herself? That didn't feel very friendly. But then she too felt a little tug of excitement. She could smell water, a lovely river smell.

The taxi stopped in front of a great arched doorway, flood-lit, with tubs of flowers on the steps. They glimpsed low buildings of pinky-yellow stone stretching away on both sides, ending in the black humps of trees pricked out by a few lights that seemed quite far away, perhaps across the invisible water.

While the driver pulled out the bags they clambered out and shook themselves straight. Magnus was still half asleep and swayed slightly as they stood waiting in the strong light while someone, dashing out, paid the taxi man and waved him goodbye. Floss half put her arm round him but she felt him shrink away. 'Sorry...' she muttered. She really must remember that he didn't like to be touched.

Then, 'My *dears*,' said a voice, 'so sorry. I had it all planned, reception committee at the station, et cett, then you got held up. *Wretched* trains.'

'I did phone,' said Sam. He was rather pleased with himself, getting the three of them safely half-way across England.

'My dear, of course you did, only then – Cecil. Well, it delayed his meal. Then I lost Arthur. Then a man from Shell telephoned, to try and book a conference – good news of course, but it made me even more behind. I just thought a taxi would be quicker. Now come in, for goodness sake. There's food all ready. The luggage can go up later. Come and get warm. It's always cold in this part of the Abbey.' She laughed. 'I'm afraid there's a price to be paid for all this antiquity. Still, we've got a good fire going.'

As they went in, under the pointed doorway, there was a click and the flood lights faded into darkness, pulling a curtain across the tantalizing theatre set of ancient glowing stone, of pillars and arches and stubby towers, of great silent trees. A huge door was pulled shut behind them and two massive bolts driven home.

'This is the original door, dears,' said the fat and friendly woman who had got to be Cousin M. 'It must be eight hundred years old, if it's a day. Now then, *food*.'

But Magnus interrupted. He said, 'I think I'd like to go straight to bed, please.'

The woman stopped, looked at the three of them, and considered. Only then, in the low, pillared entrance hall, did Magnus, Floss and Sam get their first proper look at Cousin M and she at them.

They saw a bulky, dishevelled woman of sixty wearing mud-spattered wellington boots, jeans and a baggy sweatshirt covered with meadow flowers, and the words 'Worth Protecting'. Of course, Floss was thinking, she's a gardener. That's what she does here. Cousin M had a plain no-nonsense face, a firm jaw, a straight, biggish nose and widely-spaced eyes of the most stunning dark blue. Floss envied these on the spot, and the hair too, which was still fair and extremely thick. It was gorgeous, heavy hair, the hair of an aspiring Lady Macbeth. But Cousin M obviously didn't care about it. It was tied back sensibly and caught up in an old scarf.

She saw a brother and a sister so alike they could have been two peas out of one pod – shortish and square, with the same coarse, dark hair and alert rosy faces with humour playing round the mouth. That came from their mother, her younger cousin Margaret, of whom she had always been very fond. It was great that her seaside flat had been free for their little holiday. Margaret would go picking up lame ducks though, and her latest thing was fostering this child. Cousin M wasn't at all sure about the wisdom of such an idea. Still, she liked children and these three would certainly liven the old place up.

Magnus, the foster son, was not big but he had long hands and feet which suggested he might grow tall if someone could get enough food inside him, enough sleep and enough fun… Enough *love*, love that wouldn't keep getting snatched away as he was moved from one household to the next, but poured down on him steadily, like the warmth of the sun. She knew all about what had happened to him.

'You can go to bed in two ticks, dear,' she told him, ushering them into a chilly, raftered hall hung with paintings. It was dimly lit and the pictures were not much more than dark rectangles. Light came from two standard lamps set at either end of a huge polished table which stood in front of a blazing fire laid in a grate so enormous and so elaborately carved it was like a room in its own right. A coat of arms hung above the fireplace and above that a curious black waisted clock, the shape of a legless person with a gigantic round head. It was just nine o'clock. Incongruous amid all this ancientness, was an electric food trolley on casters. Out of this Cousin M produced hot bacon sandwiches, chips and warm buns. Floss and Sam fell on the food but Magnus shook his head.

The woman studied him quietly for a minute, then she drew him gently towards her. Floss took in a sharp breath, waiting for Magnus to push the stranger away, but to her great surprise he sat beside Cousin M on the floor, meek and unprotesting, with his head against her knees. Normally, he shrank away from people, as if anyone who approached was bound to hurt him.

'Floss, Magnus and Sam… wonderful names,' Cousin M said unexpectedly, surveying them all.

Floss said shyly, 'Is your name Emily… or Emma? Mum never told us what the M was for.'

'*Emma*? Heaven's no it's – promise you won't laugh?'

They promised, even Magnus. He wasn't asleep but, from his place of safety against Cousin M's knees, was peering up at the portraits. One was much larger than the rest, the picture of a woman with very white hands and a very white face.

'My name's Maude.'

In spite of himself, Sam snorted. This was catching and Floss found herself tittering.

Cousin Maude laughed too. 'I know, it's hideous. I blame my mother, she really should have known better. She was a Maude too. She was friends with Gertrude Jekyll.'

'Jekyll and *Hyde*...' muttered Sam. It was one of the creepiest stories he had ever read, about a man who had two personalities, and whose wicked one eventually took over the good one.

'Oh no. Gertrude Jekyll was a very famous gardener. But Gertrude's a pretty hideous name too, don't you think?'

Floss said 'Well, my real name's Florence and I absolutely hate it.' She felt much reassured by Cousin Maude, they both had hideous names and they both had a weight problem. What she most liked about her was the way she was looking after Magnus, as if she understood all about his troubles and his shyness, without having to be told.

Suddenly, he came to life. 'Who's that lady?' he said, pointing to the portraits.

At first Cousin M didn't answer. It was very quiet in the vast timbered hall, no sounds but the leap of flame round burning logs, the snap of the fire and a series of clicks as the electric trolley, now unplugged, cooled down. Sam couldn't understand why it felt so cold, the fire was huge but there was a definite chill all round them.

They waited and eventually Cousin M got up, walked across the floor and pressed a switch.

A strip light over one of the paintings flickered

into life then steadied, and the three children stared. The picture was enormous, dwarfing all the others. A heavily-ornamented gilt frame, wreathed in leaves, flowers and berries, contained the full-length portrait of a young woman. She was dressed all in black except for a long white stole, like that of a priest, which was draped round her neck and fell on both sides to the hem of her dress, ending in gold fringes. She held black gloves, similarly fringed, and there was a little dog at her feet which, like her hands, looked impossibly thin and narrow.

'Is it Elizabeth the First?' said Floss. 'She's got red hair and her face is – well, it looks awfully like her.'

'No. But they *were* friends,' Cousin M said. 'The Queen stayed here, when she was young, in fact they made a special Council Chamber for her, she came so often. You can see it tomorrow. That's why there's a coat of arms over the fireplace.'

'That dog's cowering,' Sam said.

'I'm not surprised,' Floss muttered. 'She has rather a cruel face. She looks—'

'Calculating?' Cousin Maude suggested.

'Yes. That's exactly it.'

'Tell me about her,' said Magnus. Cousin M had come back to her seat by the fire. He'd moved to a rug and was sitting on it, cross-legged, staring intently into her face. What he'd said sounded a bit like a royal command and he had a fixed staring look of total concentration on his face, which Floss and Sam had become familiar with.

Cousin M looked down at him. 'I don't know very much, dear. Her first husband was much older than she was and very ambitious, I suppose that's why there's this connection with royalty – I think they had a kind of mini-court here, in the summer.'

'But *she* looks ambitious,' Floss said.

'She does. But I think she mellowed in her old age. The husband was a bit of a tyrant and I think she probably went along with it all. They do say she did things she lived to regret.'

'What things?' demanded Magnus.

Cousin M blinked up at the portrait. 'I really couldn't say, dear, it's all speculation, it all happened so long ago.'

'What happened?'

'I honestly don't know what those two got up to.' She laughed. 'I'm just the gardener round here.'

Nobody was fooled. Whatever Cousin M knew she was going to keep to herself.

Magnus's eyes followed her as she went to switch off the strip light. 'She has cruel hands,' he said, as the portrait disappeared into the shadow. 'They're like spikes.'

'It's bed time,' she said. Her voice was soft but Magnus knew it meant business. And he didn't mind at all. He felt safe with her. 'Come on,' she chivvied gently, 'we can talk about everything in the morning.'

In the entrance hall, they discovered that their pile of luggage had been removed. Cousin M looked embarrassed. 'Cecil must have taken it upstairs for you, that's good.' But she spoke as if she meant the very opposite, as if she minded that Cecil, this remote cousin of Mum's, who owned the Abbey together with Cousin M, had not bothered to come and speak to them.

'He goes to bed early,' she explained. 'He's a very early riser. He has his swim at six o'clock.'

'Can *we* swim?' Sam asked.

'Oh, I should think so. I'll have to talk to Cecil. He's in charge of that side of things. Listen, dears, I'm sorry he's gone to bed. He was annoyed with me, for getting so behind. He likes to stick to his routines. We were all up to schedule until Arthur disappeared.'

Floss suddenly remembered that this man Cecil's surname was Stickley. He *sounded* like a Stickley, like a dried-up, withered old stick. She said, 'Is Cecil our cousin as well?'

'I suppose he must be, about a million times removed,' said Cousin M, stopping at the end of a long passage way and turning left at the bottom of a staircase. On the wall, a neat modern sign said *To Turret Dormitories*.

'So Cecil's a sort of cousin,' Magnus said

slowly. He liked getting an absolutely clear picture of everything, in his mind. 'So who's Arthur?'

'My boyfriend,' Cousin M said. 'You'll see him in the morning.'

Now Magnus had seen the word 'dormitories', which suggested beds and therefore sleep, he seemed to have found a spare bit of energy and he began to climb the stairs. They were not ordinary stairs either, they were a stone spiral, enclosed within the fat tower they had seen at the corner of the Abbey buildings before the floodlights went off. He climbed quite enthusiastically, chatting a little to Cousin M. 'There is Arthur here, and there is Cecil,' he said quaintly. 'But who is that lady in the portrait?'

'Oh, don't you worry your head about her,' said Cousin M. She still seemed reluctant to say any more.

'I'm not worrying,' Magnus said firmly. 'I'd just like to know.'

'Well, her name was Alice, Lady Alice Neale. The Neale family lived here in the days of Elizabeth the First, and for quite a long time after that.'

'And *what* did you say she's supposed to have done?'

'I didn't say, dear, because I don't know.' Cousin M had gone on ahead of him, rather quickly. Her excuse was that she needed to switch more lights on.

Magnus had now got the message. There was to be no more discussion of the lady in the portrait tonight. 'Alice… it rhymes with malice…' he said, quietly, as they clumped up a third flight of twisty stairs. Then he added, but only very softly, 'It's like her hands. It's like her horrible claws.'

II

Their bedroom was on the fourth floor of the fat tower, the top room of four which lay one beneath the next like the slices of a Swiss roll. Cousin M called it a dormitory and it was one of several that had housed the children who used to come to the Abbey for very expensive courses, to learn how to play professional tennis and to swim – to Olympic standard. The children did not come any more. Cousin M said that people no longer had the spare money to pay for such things.

Magnus only knew about dormitories from school stories and so he had imagined a huge long room with rows of iron bedsteads, and a few old-fashioned wash-stands down the middle where you washed in icy-cold water while prefects hit you with bunches of twigs. His own life had been so full of torments that he was always escaping into books, where he sometimes found more. But this dormitory was just a round, low-ceilinged room with four divan beds. Each had two pillows and a plump-looking duvet covered in a blue-grey fabric with birds on, and there were screens on casters which could be rolled round each bed, to make everything more private, 'modesty screens' Cousin M called them. These were a relief to Floss. She'd not wanted to be put in a room on her own but she certainly did have her modesty.

The floor was covered in soft blue-grey carpet and the bird pattern was on the curtains too. By each bed was a white-painted locker on which stood a grey-shaded lamp. 'Sorry it's a bit on the feminine side, you two,' Cousin M said robustly to Magnus and Sam. 'We didn't decorate it like this, the company who took over the Abbey for the sports centre project absolutely insisted.'

'We don't mind, do we Mags?' said Sam. 'I expect Floss minds more. Lady Macbeth wasn't into pretty-pretty.' Floss kicked him.

'It's called "Dove". I think that's why it's these colours,' Magnus said sleepily.

They had noticed, as they'd climbed up and up, that each of the turret dormitories had the name of a bird – Eagle, Kestrel, Plover and Dove.

'There's a beautiful dovecote here,' said Cousin M, switching on the bedside lamps and turning back the duvets. 'It's unique. There isn't another like it in the whole of England.'

'Does it have a potence?' asked Magnus. He had chosen the bed by the fireplace and was pulling his screen into position, before putting his pyjamas on.

'A *what*?' Sam shouted, over the top of it.

'A potence. It's a ladder,' Magnus explained, rather pityingly, emerging a few minutes later in his night clothes. 'It revolves, so that you can go round inside and collect the eggs.'

'My goodness,' said Cousin M, admiringly, 'how on earth do you come to know a thing like that? I didn't. Someone had to tell me.'

Magnus shrugged and went back behind his screen. 'Oh, I just knew,' he muttered.

'His father was very, very clever,' Floss whispered, 'and he educated Magnus himself. He knows the most amazing things.'

Magnus came out again wearing slippers and pushed his screen back against the wall. 'There is a – a potence, Magnus,' said Cousin M. 'I'll show it to you in the morning. Or perhaps you can show it to me. It doesn't work properly. You could try mending it. I think I'll leave these windows open a bit, it really is very stuffy. You don't expect it, somehow, coming up from that chilly old hall.'

'Is the hall always chilly?' asked Magnus. 'It shouldn't be, the ceiling's quite low.' He was staring hard at Cousin M; he wanted information.

But she treated this as a casual enquiry. 'Well, I often find it a bit chilly, dear. Why?'

'I just wondered.'

'Anyhow, you'll be toasty warm up here,' she went on. 'Too hot, if anything. Now, I'm sorry about the bars, I know it makes it look a bit prison-like, but it's quite a long drop to the ground. I think this was a nursery in the old days and they usually barred the windows.'

'Actually, these bars are quite new,' Magnus said, examining them. 'Look, they've got modern screws.'

Cousin M now looked exasperated, even a little cross. She took refuge in drifting about the dormitory, straightening the bedcovers and puffing up the pillows. 'You can dump any extra things on this spare bed,' she called over from a corner. Then, 'Well now, what is *this*?'

The three of them gathered round her and looked on the fourth bed. There, neatly curled in the middle, with soft grey billows of duvet puffed up round him, was a little ginger cat. He seemed all tail and he had made a perfect circle. When he heard Cousin M, he lifted his head, blinked, yawned, mewed a little mew then buried his nose in his tail again.

'Should I take him away?' Cousin M said, stroking his ears very gently. 'He's had a big day. Caught his first mouse, by the river. That's how he got lost. He's exhausted.'

'Let him stay,' Floss begged, delighted that the bed he'd chosen was next to hers.

'All right. But I'll leave the door open, and if he's a nuisance just chuck him out. He'll find his way down to the kitchen, only he just loves *people*. And now he's got three new ones to talk to.'

'What's his name, Cousin M?' Floss could already feel herself falling in love. The cat was mildly purring in its sleep.

'Arthur.'

'But that's… your boyfriend.'

'Exactly.'

Cousin M grinned. 'Sleep tight, and God bless you all. No rush tomorrow. Get up when you like.'

'Isn't she great?' Floss whispered to the others as they lay in the dark. Arthur had already crossed over from his bed to hers, squeezed under her modesty screen and was burrowing under the duvet, settling into the special warm place in the crook of her knees. 'She's put lovely flowers in the fireplace, and everything.'

'Yes.' It sounded as if Sam was nodding off. He could smell the light, frail scent of the flowers as he lay there peacefully, and the smell of the river across the grass, and a very faint smoky smell that must be coming from the chimney flue. 'You OK, Mags?' he whispered, but there was no answer. Seconds later they both heard him snoring gently.

Somebody was crying, a sound with which Magnus was all too familiar. His mother had cried all the time after his father had walked out, and children had always cried in the Homes where he had been temporarily dumped when they first discovered how ill his mother was. Now, when babies cried in supermarkets and their mothers

31

took no notice, he couldn't stand it; he had to run away. This terror of crying seemed to be connected to an invisible main cable that went right down through the middle of him. If it were activated he felt he might die. Magnus did not understand this part of himself; all he knew was that any kind of crying was painful for him. He only ever cried in secret.

The crying was that of a woman. She had a low voice, quite deep, and she was sobbing. There were no words. He sat up in bed and his hands met warm fur. Arthur was doing his rounds, first Floss, then Sam, now him.

Magnus could just see the shape of his little head. His ears were pricked up and his fat little tail was erect and quivering. His fur was a stiff bush and he was making a curious sound, not a mew and certainly not a purr, but a kind of throaty growl, the sound of a beast that is suspicious and uncertain, possibly afraid. The low sobbing went on, though fainter now and already fading away. But the cat did not stay with Magnus. It shot off the duvet, plunged through the open door and vanished into the darkness.

It was cold in the turret room now, cold and chilly like the great hall, and Magnus's duvet felt clammy and damp. It had been hot when they'd switched their lamps off and they'd all flung their bedding aside, to get cool. The cold he now felt was like mist, in fact he could see a sort of mist in the room, lit up by some faint light. The source of this light was a mystery to him because all was dark outside; perhaps the mist had its own light. He watched it. It was like a fine piece of gauze, or a wisp of cloud, wreathing round upon itself, unfolding and refolding until, like a square of silk in the hands of a magician, it vanished into thin air leaving a coldness that was even more intense than before.

He listened again for the crying noise. It was so faint now it was no more than a sad little whisper; it had almost become part of the dissolving misty cloud. But the woman had not gone away altogether. He could still hear her, though only very faintly, and she was still in distress. Magnus decided that he must try to find her. He had to stop that crying.

But first he felt under his pillow where he always kept two things: a green army torch and a heavy black clasp knife. These things were secret treasures and absolutely nobody knew about them but him and Father Godless, who had given them to him long ago, or so it felt to Magnus.

It was awful that 'Uncle Robert', which was what Magnus had called the kind old priest, should have had the surname 'Godless' – though the old man had laughed about it. Magnus would have changed it, like people sometimes do when their name is Shufflebottom, or Smellie. He'd got to know the old man while staying with his first foster family, after they had taken him away from his mother. He was one of the priests in the church they went to. He lived in an old people's home, now, near London. but he sometimes wrote to Magnus, and occasionally sent him presents.

He'd given him the torch because he knew Magnus got scared in the dark and he'd given him a little Bible, too, with tiny print and a red silk marker. He'd called it 'the sword of the spirit which is the word of God'. But he was a very practical old man so he'd also given him the knife. This knife, like the torch and the Bible, had accompanied him on dangerous missions in the war when he'd been a soldier.

Magnus got up and felt for his dressing gown. It lay ready on his bed because he sometimes got up in the night, to go to the lavatory and, in this turret block, the main bathroom was four floors down. He liked his dressing gown. Floss's mum and dad had given it to him. He liked its bold red and blue stripes and he liked its deep pockets. Into one of these he now slid his clasp knife and into the other the little red Bible, because he was scared. The gold cross stamped deep into the front of it might give him some protection. You could wave crosses at vampires and it was supposed to shrivel them up.

He slipped through the door and made his way down the stone spiral of stairs. Each landing was lit by a small spotlight, but in between the floors there was a deep darkness. His heart bumped as he picked his way down the smooth cold treads, his ears strained for the sound of the weeping voice. He could still hear it, though it was very faint now, and it seemed to come and go as if the troubled woman was wandering about, all over this rambling place, coming near to him and then withdrawing when she did not find what she sought.

He knew where he was going and he made his way unerringly down the twisting stairs then out into the low arched entrance hall where Cousin M had greeted them. This was dimly lit by an occasional spotlight, and he could see now that there were lights in some of the flowerbeds. Through curious low windows, the shape of half-closed eyes, he could see lawns manicured with light-dark stripes where the mower had gone up and down, and the glint of shifting water and the great trees standing like silent sentinels.

The door to the Great Hall where Cousin M had fed them was ajar, but only a crack. Magnus pushed at it and the vast slab of whorled timber, many centimetres thick and patterned with marvellous iron traceries, swung open silently. Then it gave a single, sharp creak a sound not particularly loud but deafening in the vast room hung with its rows of gilded portraits. At the table, by the fire where they had eaten their sandwiches, a man sat in front of a chessboard. At the creak of the hinges he turned his head sharply and, seeing the small boy in the doorway, got abruptly to his feet, sending two of the chess pieces rolling across the floor. He touched a bank of switches by the fireplace and lights came on everywhere. Magnus was terrified but he stood his ground as the elderly man, who walked with a slight limp, strode purposefully towards him.

It was his first meeting with Colonel Stickley, the mysterious relative of Cousin M's who had gone off to bed without greeting them. Magnus never forgot that moment, the tall spindly figure limping across the cold chequered floor, the sudden harsh light after the reassuring darkness, and what that light revealed – row upon row of faces, priests and soldiers, men in university robes posed self-importantly over open books, women in wimples, children playing with cats and dogs and with curious toys, such as you only ever saw in museums. So many faces looking down upon the modern man and the modern boy, each from their own little corner in the greater sweep of history. But the face he had come to see was not among them. The huge gold frame, containing cruel Lady Alice of the thin white hands, was empty. He found himself looking up at a blank black rectangle.

Did the Colonel see? Magnus could not decide because, instantly, the old man had interposed his own tall, stooping figure between the boy and the painting, had bent down and thrust his whiskery face at him. 'Humph! What's this? Are you sleep-walking or something?

Magnus, smelling pipe smoke and whisky, suddenly burst into tears. The crying of the woman which had brought him here had most definitely ceased now, and the painting was most definitely blank. These two things belonged together, of that he felt certain. But *how* they belonged he did not understand. She had looked so cruel, the Lady Alice Neale. It could surely not have been Lady Alice that wept. But where had she gone to, slipping out of her gilded frame and leaving the canvas empty? None of it made sense. He suddenly felt bewildered and lost, and he very much wanted to go back to bed.

The Colonel looked down at the snivelling boy, inspecting him through small round spectacles as, Magnus felt, one might scrutinise some botanical specimen under glass. Then, very awkwardly and stiffly, he stretched out his hand and laid it lightly on the boy's shoulder. 'Stay there young man' he said, then he went round the hall switching off all the main lights. Magnus could hear him talking to himself, he seemed to be complaining about Maude. 'Mad woman, my cousin. What did she want to put you up there for, four floors up? I told her not to but the woman wouldn't listen. It's not civilised. No wonder you lost your bearings. Come on, I'll have you in bed in two shakes of a donkey's tail. I'm going to see about this in the morning, get you moved. Are you up to walking up all those wretched stairs? Want a fireman's lift? My son always liked a fireman's lift, cheeky little beggar.'

Magnus suspected that a fireman's lift, one of the few terms with which he was not familiar, involved being carried back to his room over the old man's shoulder. 'I'm all right,' he said firmly. 'I'd just like to go back to bed. Sorry if I frightened you.'

The Colonel gave a dry laugh. 'You didn't frighten me, young man, I often sit up late. Can't sleep y'know, it's my age. All right then, follow me, and mind where you put your feet, the lighting's not good along these corridors.'

But as they left the hall something made Magnus look back. He said, 'You've left one of the lights on.'

Colonel Stickley turned round. 'So I have, and the Lady Alice won't like *that*. Beautiful young woman but she had quite a temper, they say, quite an old paddy.' He clicked a switch and Magnus saw the tall woman in white and black with the thin little dog at her feet fade into the darkness.

As they went along the corridors towards the turret stairs, he saw two tapestries hanging on a wall, lit by a solitary lamp. One portrayed Pontius Pilate washing his hands in a bowl of water. A soldier stood by with a scarlet towel and Jesus, in a corner and already wearing his crown of thorns, was looking on, sadly. The other showed a scene from the Old Testament. Father Robert had told him the story, about Balaam's donkey who was beaten because he disobeyed his master. Knowing that he was in the presence of an angel of God, the poor beast had lain down in the road and would not budge. Here, in ragged, faded threads, was that donkey, flattened, with its ears sticking out at right angles, as if something had run over it, and a great ball of shimmering light that was the angel. It was only a glimpse as the Colonel, puffing slightly, started to mount the spiral stairs, but it made Magnus think of Arthur, the little cat. Animals were sometimes more sensitive to the big, deep things than human beings were, and Arthur had been plainly terrified when the crying began. Like Balaam's ass, the cat must have suddenly picked up a very strong presence, and he had fled from it. It was definitely not good, like the angel, but perhaps it was not totally bad either. All Magnus knew for certain was that it was very troubled. Its grief was great and it had wept human tears.

But how could it have anything to do with that hard-faced woman in the gold frame, the woman who had, he was sure, been *out* of it when he'd first come into the great hall and found the Colonel playing chess? And had Colonel Stickley known that the woman had gone from the frame and was that gruff, calm treatment of Magnus all a sham?

As the Colonel said goodnight to him and he snuggled down into his bed again, he once more felt afraid. He wanted some arms round him. Why hadn't he gone to Majorca with Auntie Win and Uncle Donald? He felt round in the bed. Perhaps Arthur had crept back and was waiting for him, a warm purry presence, but the cat was not there. So he turned on his side, burrowing down as Colonel Stickley limped down the stairs, still muttering to himself. 'Flowers in the fireplace,' Magnus heard. 'Whatever next... for three children. Is this the Hilton Hotel? Humph, I'm not clearing the mess up. It'll be that damned cat.'

But a cat as small as Arthur could not have achieved the complete wreckage that now lay in the grate, a wreckage Magnus had not seen as he'd climbed thankfully and hurriedly into his bed. Cousin M's beautiful arrangement of white peonies, set in the fireplace in their honour, lay in ruins. The simple green vase that had held them was smashed and it looked as if some of the smaller pieces of glass had been ground into powder. The flowers themselves had been torn from their stalks and dismembered, petal by petal, and they lay upon the dark polished floor of the tower room like big flakes of snow.

III

Cousin M, coming into the turret room next morning, saw the flowers scattered in the grate, knelt down and, without comment, began to pick them up.

'It wasn't me, I didn't knock them over,' Magnus said defensively, sitting up in bed. He'd become very used to people telling him off for things he hadn't done.

Cousin M showed no reaction. 'It's all right, dear. It's a shame about the vase though, it was a pretty one. Perhaps the children's mother could get me another. It came from the old glass factory near my flat in Majorca.'

Sam and Floss had woken up too. Through the barred window they could see a square of cloudless blue sky, sun shining on a sheet of water. The day suddenly felt good.

'Don't know if you're interested, but there's breakfast down below,' Cousin M said casually, tidying the bits of glass into a heap. 'Mind you don't cut yourselves on this. I'll bring a dustpan.'

'Did Arthur knock the flowers over?' asked Floss.

'Probably. He doesn't know his own strength, that animal.' But Magnus, who was observing her very carefully, didn't believe a word of it. It was quite obvious to him that this kind of thing must have happened before and she'd got used to it. Her studied matter-of-factness did not fool him at all.

'I'm *very* interested in breakfast,' announced Sam, suddenly smelling a faint bacon smell which he decided must be coming up the chimney flue. The sandwiches and buns of the night before now seemed a very long time ago.

'Well, get ready and come down. We'll be in the hall. When there are just the two of us we usually eat in the kitchen but you're a good excuse to do things properly. I'm afraid the Colonel doesn't like the way I slob around in my gardening things.'

While they were cleaning their teeth, Floss said to Sam 'Do you think Mags is all right?'

'Seems to be. Why?'

'I'm sure he was crying again, in the night. It woke me up.'

Sam shrugged, then made a great business of rinsing and spitting. He half-believed that a noise had woken him too, the voice of someone in distress. It hadn't sounded at all like Magnus, it had sounded too adult. But he was a very sound sleeper and he had finally concluded that he was almost certainly dreaming. He'd snuggled down in the bed until he'd fallen asleep again.

Floss had lain awake for some time too, but the sound she'd thought was Magnus had faded away in the end. The other thing she remembered was feeling very cold. 'Do you think Cousin M has got any hot water bottles?' she said, as they climbed back up to Dove, to collect Magnus for breakfast. 'My feet were like ice, last night.'

'You could ask her,' said Sam. Then he added 'My feet were cold too. I put some socks on. It's funny, how it suddenly went very cold. It was cold down in the Great Hall as well. And yet our dormitory's a warm little room compared with the others, according to Cousin M. That's why she's put us up there. She said that Colonel Stickley was cross about it, apparently. He told her off. He said we should have been in one of the portakabins.'

The long oak table by the fireplace was set for breakfast with a checked cloth and neatly folded napkins. As Cousin M seated them all Colonel Stickley came in with a loaded tray. He presented an interesting contrast with Cousin M who was wearing her grubby gardening clothes of the night before. He looked very formal and very smart in a tweed suit with a waistcoat and a watch chain across it, a silk handkerchief tucked into the top pocket and brown brogue shoes polished to a mirror gloss. 'He's a bit of a smoothie, isn't he?' Sam whispered to Floss, as they sat down. 'What is he doing frying breakfast for us lot? Don't they have servants in a place like this? Where's the cook?'

Cousin M said, sticking spoons into pots of honey and marmalade and manhandling a very large tea pot, 'Let's have a few introductions. Cecil, this is Sam, Floss and Magnus. This is Colonel Stickley, children.'

Embarrassed, and unused to formal introductions, the three of them made vague mumbling noises and took refuge in their bowls of cornflakes. 'Stick insect,' thought Sam, watching the colonel's long legs arrange themselves neatly under the table. The old man did not smile, not did he look in their direction. The business of the moment was breakfast and he was concentrating on that.

Magnus, who was sitting with his back to the fireplace, thought he knew why Colonel Stickley was ignoring them all. It was because of the episode the night before. He'd been quite friendly in the end, in a stiff, grandfatherly way, helping him up to bed, but he was very different this morning. Magnus was determined to talk to him in private but he would have to find the right moment.

He chewed his cornflakes and ran his eyes along the rows of portraits. The Lady Alice Neale, in her black dress, was back in her frame. There were the thin, unkind lips and the cruel hands, there was the little dog. He did not dare look from

44

the portrait to Colonel Stickley. It was obviously better for now to go along with the pretence that the two of them had never met before.

Instead he said 'Who is the big fat man?'

Colonel Stickley glanced along the rows of painted faces and removed a sliver of food from between his teeth. 'His nickname is Burst Belly,' he said. 'He was a monk, head of this place, once. He was in charge of the Black Canons. Henry the Eighth got rid of them and he didn't much like it. So he put a curse on the Abbey, or so people say.'

Floss and Sam looked up at Burst Belly too. He was a huge and ugly man wearing the black and white robes of a priest. The white part of the costume was lacy and frilled like a Victorian night gown, incongruous under the flat silver cross which hung round his neck.

'Good name for him, wasn't it, Burst Belly,' Cousin M remarked, buttering her toast thickly and heaping on the marmalade. 'He obviously ate too much, like me. I do love food, don't you?'

Floss said 'I don't like his face. It doesn't look exactly… well, *holy*, to me. It's not the kind of expression you expect in a priest. Did he really curse the Abbey?'

'That's the story,' said Colonel Stickley. 'But who knows? It's certainly had a sad history. If you look at all the families that have lived here, you'll see that nobody stayed around for very long. Things tended to happen to people.'

'What sorts of things?' demanded Magnus, and his voice was unnaturally high and shrill. It was the voice he unconsciously seemed to develop when he was really concentrating on something. It irritated the other two.

'Shh, Mags,' said Floss, and pressed his foot under the table.

But Magnus seemed not to have heard. 'That's what *you* told us,' he informed Cousin M.

Cousin M blinked at him. 'Me, dear? What did I tell you? I'm afraid you'll have to remind me.'

'You said yesterday that Lady Alice did things she lived to regret; that's exactly what you said, those were your exact words.'

Floss was now pressing down on Magnus's feet just as hard as she could because she knew it was a dangerous moment. If they didn't somehow change course, he would start crying, possibly even screaming. It had happened just once or twice, and it was frightening. It seemed to be something to do with the stresses of the awful life he'd had, shut away in the unfamiliar house with his sick mother, wondering what had happened to his father.

But Colonel Stickley, not knowing what was going on under the table, actually helped matters by glaring at Cousin M, rolling up his napkin and standing up. 'End of subject,' he announced crisply. 'Now then, I have a very busy morning, but if you're prepared to come with me now I will show you a little of the Abbey, so you can get your bearings for the day.'

Cousin M said in a nervous voice, 'Why don't you let them go round on their own, Cecil? You've so much else to do and I'm sure they'd be happier poking round independently.'

Sam said, 'We'll be fine, sir, we won't touch anything'. He was dying to get away from Colonel Stickley.

'*I* shall take you round,' he said frostily. '"Poking about", as you call it, is precisely what I do not wish to encourage, and he produced a bunch of keys from his pocket. 'The public still use this place from time to time, Maude, in spite of our present circumstances. There are all kinds of hazards in an old building like this. I'd like them to see exactly what's what.'

'Very well, Cecil,' Maude said meekly, then, to the children, 'I'll be in my garden this morning, dears, if you want me. It's the walled garden, beyond the dovecote at the end of the Long Walk. Otherwise, see you at lunch.'

'At twelve-thirty,' said Colonel Stickley, 'and it's… nine o'clock now'. He consulted a large gold pocket watch, tapped it and dropped it back into his waistcoat pocket. 'I will meet you in the entrance hall in ten minutes, after you've rinsed off your breakfast crumbs. I shall go and do the same.'

Floss and Sam exchanged disappointed looks,

shrugged silently at each other, then set off obligingly for their turret room. But Magnus lingered. In between the pictures of Burst Belly and the Lady Alice Neale was a tiny portrait of a young boy. Magnus hadn't noticed it the night before but now sunshine was filtering through small leaded panes and a square of barred light was shining on it. He was almost certain that it was a boy, though the child was very prettily dressed in a lacy ruff and had longish golden curls. Between two fingers he held a white, many-petalled flower.

Magnus said, 'Is that a peony?'

The Colonel glanced up at the little painting. 'I wouldn't know. Flowers are Maude's department. *Why?*' he demanded quite sharply. 'I must say you ask rather a lot of questions.'

Magnus was not put off. He was collecting information. 'Well, she put some flowers like that in our room, and the cat knocked them over and broke the vase. Where is Arthur, by the way?'

'I'm sure I don't know. Cats aren't my department, young man. Asleep somewhere, I suppose, it's a nice life. I must get on, I've a great deal to do this morning. Rinsed your hands, have you?'

Ignoring this Magnus said, 'Who is that boy in the painting? *Is* it a boy?'

'It is. And we don't know. He might have been a son of the Lady Alice. She was married twice and she had several children. If it is a son of hers, then he wasn't born here. He's not in the parish records, and he's not included in the family memorial, down in the church. Seen the church have you? Rinsed your hands?' he repeated.

'Just going to,' muttered Magnus, but he didn't. His hands were perfectly clean. Instead he went into the entrance hall and stood by the tapestries, Balaam's donkey and its meeting with the angel, Pontius Pilate washing away his guilt. That set him thinking about the woman in the night again, the woman who'd cried, and about the misty coldness, and how Arthur had fled in terror. Who *was* the pretty child with the flower between his fingers, and who had smashed Cousin M's vase of green glass and torn her peonies to pieces? He had come to a conclusion about Cousin Maude and Colonel Stickley. They were both pretending. Both of them knew that all was not well in the Abbey but neither of them was prepared to say anything. This thought rather excited Magnus, but it also made him afraid. He'd quite like to talk to Floss and Sam about it, but would they laugh at him? He suspected that the best person to talk to would be Colonel Stickley, if he could get him on his own, and in a good mood – if the old man ever had such things.

Colonel Stickley was obviously determined to show them as little as possible of 'his' Abbey.

He'd made it clear at the beginning that he thought of it as his, even though Mum had told them that it was Cousin M's money which had saved it from being sold. It was obvious that they were not to see a lot of the rooms.

'What's in *there*?' they kept asking, as he hustled them past intriguing doors bristling with ancient nails and bolts, and very firmly shut. 'Can we just have a peep?'

'Absolutely nothing of interest,' the Colonel would say or 'just household rubbish', or 'the domestic offices'. And the faster he hurried them on the more they wanted to linger and to explore.

What they saw were the public or 'show' rooms; those rooms which were on view to possible clients, for firms to use when they held conferences at the Abbey – a money-making scheme which, like the sports centre, had almost ground to a halt.

'Why don't people come any more?' asked Magnus.

Floss glared at him and Sam tried to get near enough to give him a kick. 'Don't keep going on about it, Mags, it's tactless,' he whispered, holding him back as Colonel Stickley unlocked a door labelled 'Council Chamber'.

But Colonel Stickley had heard. 'Ask away,' he said. 'We're in a recession, young man, everybody is tightening their belts. People don't have the money for luxuries any more. Our charges are high, naturally, because we give a very high quality of service, but there isn't the money to pay for it. QED,' he added.

'"As has been demonstrated,"' said Magnus. '"*Quod erat demonstrandum*".'

'Stop showing off,' Floss hissed at him. 'It's getting on my nerves.' In the atmosphere of the Abbey Magnus definitely seemed to be coming out of his shell and to be more confident. He was talking more and asking most of the questions. She supposed this was better than sitting in silence all the time but she was finding it irritating, particularly when he paraded his knowledge in front of Colonel Stickley.

But the old man didn't seem to have heard. 'I don't mind the place being empty for a few months,' he said. 'I quite like it to myself, actually. All those tennis-playing brats were beginning to get me down.'

'Thanks a lot,' mouthed Sam to Floss, as they stepped inside a large panelled room on one wall of which was a small bay window with a cushioned seat and a view of the river. There was another huge fireplace with a coat of arms above it.

'This room was improved,' he told them, 'for the young Elizabeth the First. She was a friend of Lady Alice Neale. It's not very likely she held councils here, but that's why they enlarged it, just in case.'

'What a waste,' said Sam. He disapproved of the Royal Family. 'It's like putting new lavatories into places when the Queen's only going to be there for about five minutes.'

'But even royalty has to go to the lavatory,' Magnus observed solemnly.

Floss started to laugh but the Colonel didn't seem to notice. 'They raised the floor in this room,' he said. 'It would have been much lower, originally. They really did do their best to get the Court to come here. They were obviously very ambitious, and it worked. The husband became a major diplomat. Anyhow, that's about it, really. Pleasant room for a spot of reading or sewing, not to mention the royal comings and goings. Come along then, we'll do the lower floor next.'

Floss and Sam set off in front of him. They were bored with these empty rooms. 'Do you think we could slip away?' Sam suggested. 'He's obviously not going to show us much else. I'd rather come back when he's out of the way, when he goes off to London or something.' The gardens and the river looked much more tempting than this series of empty rooms and, so far as he was concerned, the sooner the grand tour was over the better.

As the Colonel pulled the heavy door shut behind them, Magnus, hanging back for a final peek, was aware of a rush of cold air. It was not the general cold of an ancient, thick-walled dwelling, that retained its delicious coolness on a day of sun, it was a more precise, sharp cold; it was enclosed in time, like a phrase of music, or a sentence. And he distinctly saw, as the closing door filled the sunlit space beyond, the figure of a woman moving across the Council Chamber from right to left. Her Elizabethan dress was pure white and round her neck hung a broad, black priest-like stole. She was carrying white gloves and she continually twisted them in her hands, as if they were a handkerchief. He could hear a sobbing noise. He was unable to see the apparition's feet. These were cut off from his view above the ankle, as if the rest of her was moving along at a lower level, about a foot below his eye.

Magnus cried out, then clapped his hand across his mouth. The Colonel looked down sharply. 'You all right, young man? Got a pain? Shouldn't bolt your food, you know.'

He said, 'You've just locked somebody in. There's somebody in there, a woman. Listen, she's crying, can't you hear her?'

Colonel Stickley stared at him, grimaced, pulled at his moustache then stood very still. The sound, though muffled through the thick oak door, was the same sound that had woken him in the night, the anguished sound of inconsolable weeping that Magnus had been unable to bear. And he could not bear it now. He clapped his hands to his ears and screamed, 'Stop it! Stop it, can't you!'

The Colonel dropped his bunch of keys and

shook him vigorously. 'Come on now, no hysterics, there's no need for that.' But his voice was quite gentle. This was the foster child, the boy whose father had walked out, never to be heard of again, and whose mother had lost her mind, the child who'd never had a childhood. 'Wait there,' he said, and he limped off after Floss and Sam. 'I just have to oil a lock,' he called after them. 'Make your way down to the buttery. We'll be with you in a jiffy.'

Coming back to Magnus he picked up his keys, unlocked the door of the Council Chamber and steered him into the room. 'See for yourself,' he said, 'go on, investigate. Climb up the chimney and pull up the floor boards. It's all been done before, you know.' His voice, no longer brisk and soldierly, was wavering, that of a tired old man. It was almost as if *he* wanted to cry now.

Magnus stared into the room though he knew perfectly well that he would not see the woman in white. She belonged to another time, to a time when the floor of the Council Chamber had been lower. She had been walking on *that* floor which was why she had seemed to him to have no feet. These were the simple mechanics of ghosts. Magnus knew all about them from old Father Robert, whose church had once been inhabited by an unhappy spirit which he had laid to rest with his prayers. The mechanics were not what scared him, they were just about two kinds of time getting muddled up. What was frightening was how he felt about the two women – the one who had cried in the night and the one he had just seen gliding across this room. Each spectre had brought the awful coldness with her, a cold that went into his very marrow and felt like death. And the coldness was part of her pain, of the grief which troubled her so. In a way he didn't fully understand, it was as if her pain had joined itself to his. He was suffering as well, which was why he'd had to stop the noise of the crying.

Were there two women or were they one and the same person – the woman in the night, who he believed must have been Lady Alice, because her frame had stood empty, and now this other woman, all in white? Magnus could not begin to work out what was happening. He felt as if the top of his head was coming off, through too much thinking.

A hand descended on to his shoulder. 'As you see,' Colonel Stickley informed him, 'the room really is empty. There is nothing going on here and there never has been. All this talk of ghosts is all silly rumour, put about by people who are trying to ruin my business because they want to get this place from me. Do you understand, boy… what's your name?'

'Magnus.'

'Do you understand, Magnus? Do we understand… each other?'

'Yes.' Then he added, because he felt that Colonel Stickley was very afraid, and lonely, 'sir'.

Inside, he wanted to challenge the Colonel, but how could he say, 'Actually, you're a liar and so is Cousin M.' He felt sorry for him and he knew he was only trying to protect them, probably hoping this bit of ghostly activity would die down, which was what sometimes happened. Magnus knew quite a bit about ghosts. Father Godless had made a study of them, after the episode in his church, and one thing he'd discovered was that ghosts who've been quiet for centuries sometimes are often activated by children. There'd been lots of children coming to the Abbey, to do sports courses, then they'd gone away. Now he'd arrived, with Flossie and Sam. Was it *their* presence that had started things up again? More particularly, was it *his*? He asked himself this question, not because he was special – Magnus hadn't felt special to anybody for a very long time – but because he had a feeling that the two women, if there were two, might be trying to tell him something.

'Good man,' the Colonel grunted, and locked up again. 'Let's go down to the buttery,' he said, resuming his normal, crusty, old-soldier voice, and he led the way towards the stairs.

Floss and Sam were waiting for them in the entrance hall. 'We couldn't find the steps down,' Floss said, but Magnus knew that this wasn't true.

She had decided she ought to wait for him. Now she caught hold of his hand. 'You OK, Mags? You look cold. You've got goose-pimples.'

He hesitated. 'I'm OK, but I thought I saw someone in that room, that Council Chamber. We went back.' He wanted to say, 'It was a woman dressed in white and she had no feet'. But he felt he'd made a kind of promise to Colonel Stickley so instead he said, 'Anyhow, there wasn't anybody. It was just so bright in that room. I suppose the light comes off the river, I suppose that was it.'

'Yes, that would be it,' Floss said reassuringly, but she could not quite look him in the eyes, and Magnus had the feeling that she, too, was pretending – that they were all pretending, with each other.

IV

The buttery was the old name for the kitchens. To get to these they passed through a series of low-ceilinged rooms which ran into each other through a series of shallow arches, the roofs propped up here and there by stubby columns. This part of the Abbey had more the feel of a crypt than a dwelling house, but it smelt of stale cigarettes and gravy. There was a Coke machine in one corner, a row of pay phones and a lot of plastic tables and chairs.

Sam was very excited. 'This part's really *ancient*,' he said, poking at the knobbled walls. 'Can't you just see those Black Canons down here, Burst Belly tearing meat off a spit and chucking his bones through the window? Pity about the machines.'

Colonel Stickley seemed to respond to this enthusiasm. 'I know, but it's what the modern world demands, I'm afraid. Anyhow, I might get them ripped out. We don't need them any more.

Hmmm. This house should be restored to its former glory.'

The windows in these rooms were almost on a level with people's feet. Through them you could see the river sliding past and beyond the river unfolded an endless vista of fields and woods, basking in the steady light of another perfect day. A fly buzzed. It was going to be very hot.

In the buttery kitchen a small muscular-looking man in long khaki shorts stood frying something at an Aga cooker. At his feet, curled up in a basket, slept Arthur. The basket had toys in it – a blue mouse, some ping-pong balls and a fluffy black spider.

'Morning, Wilf,' said Colonel Stickley.

'Morning, Sir,'

The man in shorts stuck his rubber spatula in the air as a kind of salute, clicked his heels together and went on frying.

'These are Maude's young relations,' said Colonel Stickley. 'Er, what are your names?' He was irritable again. They couldn't keep up with his moods.

'Floss.'

'Magnus.'

'Sam.'

They spoke dutifully, in turn, feeling like the Three Wise Monkeys, and Floss knelt down by the cat basket and tickled Arthur's ears.

'Pleased to meet you,' said Wilf. 'Hope you

enjoyed your breakfast. I'm just about to have mine.'

'Oh, *you* cooked it,' said Floss. 'We thought it was the Colonel—'

'He's Front of House,' explained Wilf. 'I'm your man. Want some more? There's plenty going.'

'I wouldn't say no,' began Sam, his mouth watering at the sight of a pan of scrambled eggs. But Colonel Stickley was making it very clear that the official tour of the Abbey was over. He had produced a clipboard and a pen.

'Plans for the day, Wilf,' he muttered, unfolding some spectacles.

'Yes, sir,' said Wilf, clicking his heels again.

'We muster at twelve-thirty for a light luncheon,' the Colonel told the three children. 'Until then, a very good morning to you. You may have the run of the grounds and gardens, although anywhere closed to you is, naturally *closed*. I may trust you, I hope?'

'Yes, Colonel Stickley,' they all said in chorus. They hadn't meant to, at all, they didn't like being treated like infants. But he was that kind of person; it was best to humour him.

'His "luncheon" means, cheese-and-pickle sarnies made by yours truly,' whispered Wilf. 'See you around.' And he grinned at them.

Unexpectedly dismissed, they trailed up the stairs

again and found themselves back in the entrance hall with its tapestries of Balaam's donkey and Pontius Pilate washing his hands. The front door stood open and they went through on to the gravelled drive where the taxi had deposited them the night before. Directly in front of them stretched a long lawned walk, edged by huge trees, and at the end of this they could see tall walls of dark brick. To one side was a circular building with a conical roof and some tiny dormer windows. 'That must be the dovecote,' said Sam, 'it's huge… and there's the walled garden. Come on!' He wanted to explore it all now, without Colonel Stickley breathing down his neck.

'Think I'd like to go and put something cooler on first,' Floss said. 'It's fantastically hot. If we got our swimming things, do you think we'd be allowed in the pool?'

'It's worth a try, if it's not locked,' Sam answered.

'Let's go back upstairs for a bit,' Magnus said. 'I've got to talk to you. It's urgent.'

The other two looked at him, then at each other. It wasn't a bit like Magnus to take the initiative. He usually did whatever the other two suggested.

'Talk to us about what, Mags?'

He looked round cautiously. 'Everything. Let's go to the dormitory, where we can be private.'

The bedroom was very stuffy, in spite of its open windows, and the lawns below were starting to go brown. They looked dried-up at the edges. 'This is definitely a heatwave,' said Floss, pulling a baggy T-shirt and some shorts out of her suitcase. After inspecting the shorts, she put them back. They were last year's and quite tight. They would cling to her bottom and make her hotter than ever. Instead, she selected a long cotton skirt. She would float round the Abbey in it and pretend to be Lady Macbeth, even if she didn't audition for the play next term.

'"Had he not resembled my father, as he slept, I had done it…"' she murmured, dreamily. Magnus stared at her. 'That's *Macbeth*,' she informed him rather proudly. 'You see, even Lady Macbeth had some human feelings. She couldn't actually bring herself to murder King Duncan in the end, so she made her husband do it.'

'I know it's *Macbeth*,' replied Magnus quite irritably. 'Killing Duncan affected her the most. Macbeth turned into a kind of monster, but she went steadily mad. She just couldn't forget what they'd done, all that wringing of hands, all that trying to wash the blood away. "Canst thou not minister to a mind diseased, Pluck from the memory a rooted sorrow?"' he whispered. 'Nobody could help her, they did try.'

There was a silence then, because tears had come into his eyes and Floss realised that Magnus was really speaking about his own mother. She wanted to put her arms round him but she didn't dare. It all felt too private.

Instead, she clapped him rather too heartily on the back. 'Magnus,' she said breezily, 'the things you know. You amaze me. I've been doing *Macbeth* for weeks and you never let on that you knew all that.'

'Well, I don't know much,' he said modestly, 'but Father Godless took me to it, in London. It was in a park, in the open air. I read bits of it afterwards, on my own. I suppose I just remembered those lines.' Then he added, 'And that's what I want to talk to you about. I think the women here are a bit like Lady Macbeth.'

'What women?' Sam said, sitting on his bed. 'There aren't any women, apart from Cousin M.' He was feeling a bit excluded by all this talk about Shakespeare between his sister and Magnus.

'Yes there are. Haven't you heard them?'

'Heard what? What are you on about, Mags? Why do you have to talk in riddles?'

Floss glared at him. They both knew that Magnus could be very unpredictable and that you sometimes had to tread carefully with him, especially when something really upset him. It was fantastic that he'd done as much talking as he had, since they'd arrived at the Abbey. It could only be because they were on their own, away from the grown-ups. But if Sam bullied him he'd go back into his shell and clam up for the rest of the holiday. He was an extremely fragile person and he'd just made it very clear to them how much his mother's sufferings were preying on his mind.

He sat cross-legged on his divan, put the tips of his fingers together and brought his hands to his mouth. Then he looked up at the other two and said, 'Do you believe in ghosts?'

'No.' Sam answered first, firmly and loudly, without hesitation.

'Why not?'

'Because, well, I don't know why not. Except that there are usually quite good explanations for them, most of the time.'

'What kind of explanations?'

'Well, for example – in houses that make noises in the night. It's usually something like central-heating pipes, that kind of thing.'

Magnus was unimpressed. 'What else?' he said. 'That's not much to go on.'

'I don't know what else. I just don't believe in ghosts and actually, I'm not very interested in them.' For some reason Sam was feeling threatened.

'But you're interested in history.'

'Well, so what?'

'History's about ghosts.'

'It's not. It's about time.'

'Same thing,' said Magnus. 'What about you, Floss? Do you think ghosts are a load of rubbish too? It's obvious your brother does.'

She said nothing at first. Sam wouldn't like this

remark and neither did she. Eventually she said rather coldly, 'I've never seen a ghost, Magnus, but that's not to say I don't believe.'

'Why are you asking us, anyhow?' Sam said irritably. 'And why are you being so rude? Would you mind getting to the point? We're not all as intellectual as you, Magnus, and I must say you're extremely good at making people feel small.'

Magnus blushed. There was an atmosphere now. This was the nearest the three of them had ever come to quarrelling.

'I'm sorry,' he said in a small voice, but Sam had stalked across to the window and was staring moodily through the bars. Magnus looked taken aback. Sam had always been so kind to him, they both had. 'I've said I'm sorry,' he repeated. His father, whom he didn't remember very well any more, had always said that if you apologised then that was it, that the other person had to accept it. 'Can't we be friends?' he pleaded, realising that he really minded Sam ignoring him, and that both Sam and Floss were very important to him, and that he needed them to stick up for him.

But Sam went on staring through the window. Floss walked over to him and whispered something that Magnus couldn't hear, then a prolonged and muffled conversation took place.

'*OK*,' he heard finally. 'But stop going on about it!' And Sam, red-faced and fierce-looking, turned back into the room then came and flopped down on his bed. 'Go on, Mags,' he said. 'You were saying, about whether ghosts exist or not. Why are you so uptight about it all?'

Magnus hesitated. He was nervous now, in case Sam shouted again. 'Do you really want to know?' he asked cautiously.

'Yes, I really want to know,' replied Sam in an expressionless voice.

'Well all right. I think there's something wrong with this house, something seriously wrong. I felt it as soon as we arrived.'

Sam pulled a face. 'Well, that's not new. There's lots wrong, I'd say, but it's got nothing to do with ghosts.'

'All right, what *is* wrong?' asked Floss. She hadn't managed to talk to their mother about Cousin M and the Abbey, but she knew that Sam had, after the booklet arrived.

He said, 'Well, it's all a bit mysterious. According to Mum the Colonel's obviously spent a load of money on this place, in the past I mean, trying to make a profit out of it, so that he can carry on living here. But it's all come to nothing, and now Cousin M's had to bale him out. People obviously don't use it for conferences, and they don't do any sports training here, either. It feels as if the whole place is in limbo to me. And who looks after it? There's nobody around much, except that old man Wilf. Cousin M does the garden and the Colonel just, well, fusses around saying he's busy.'

'There's something evil about the place, that's the reason,' said Magnus, with complete authority. 'People must have been put off by something, they must be too frightened to come here. Cousin M told us that the Colonel always went to bed early, but he was awake, in the middle of the night, and he was still fully dressed. He was playing chess by the fire. He obviously can't sleep. His worries keep him awake.'

'And what were *you* doing wandering round in the night?' Sam asked suspiciously.

Magnus hesitated. Sam had already dismissed ghosts, relegating them to creaking water pipes. But Floss felt more sympathetic. He had a choice. He could either pretend that all was well, like Colonel Stickley did, or he could take Floss and Sam into his confidence. He liked them and he very much wanted them to like him. He'd never been part of a proper family before.

He took the plunge. 'Something woke me up,' he said, 'a woman.'

'Did you see anything?'

'No. I just heard her. She was crying. And this room – it went terribly cold and it, sort of, filled with mist. It felt just like it did when we went into the great hall, cold all of a sudden, and for no reason. The cat was asleep on my bed but it woke up, and it went rigid. He was really terrified, honestly and he ran away.'

Floss put her hand on his arm. "OK. Well, that's interesting because we were cold too. Weren't we, Sam?"

'Yeah,' Sam said, grudgingly. 'But that doesn't mean anything. This is a tower room, for heaven's sake. Look how thick the walls are.'

'Yes, but it's one of the warmer rooms, according to Cousin M, that's why she put us here, in spite of Colonel Stickley telling her not to. You told us that yourself,' Floss reminded him.

'That's true, I admit that,' Sam said reluctantly. He *had* been woken up by the sound of somebody crying and he knew that it hadn't been Magnus. The voice had been grown-up, and female.

'I went down to the picture gallery,' Magnus went on, 'you know, the hall where we had the sandwiches. That's where the Colonel was, playing a chess game with himself. And when I looked at that big portrait, the one of the woman—' But he stopped. They were not going to believe this.

'*What*?'

'She wasn't there.'

Sam's mouth curled. 'What do you mean, "she wasn't there"?'

'Exactly what I say. The picture frame was empty. The canvas was blank, as if someone had rubbed her out.'

'So she was… walking around the place? Is that what you're saying?' Sam was starting to sound hostile again.

'I don't know. I'm just telling you what I saw. I wasn't asleep, I was down there and that's what had happened. I'd swear on a Bible, if you wanted me to.'

There was a long silence. This was utterly serious. Magnus often talked of an 'Uncle Robert' who'd been a priest and had been kind to him. It was because of this old man that he sometimes talked of 'swearing on the Bible'. It wasn't a thing he ever said lightly. Floss, now seeing in her own mind's eye the enormous gilded frame empty of the haughty young woman who had stood there, so imperious and proud, felt suddenly frightened herself. They had all agreed that the Lady Alice Neale looked cold, almost cruel. And yet her ghost had wept as it wandered about.

'You said *women*,' Sam reminded him, but rather more quietly than before, as if he too felt a bit frightened – or at least, less certain. 'So are there more of these wandering ghosts?'

'I don't know,' Magnus answered. 'But there was definitely somebody in the Council Chamber just now. You two had gone downstairs and I stayed with the Colonel while he locked up because, well, you never know, and I *saw* something. I thought at first that it was the Lady Alice, she had the same kind of Elizabethan ruff and she was tall and thin. But then I realised it couldn't be, because she was dressed in white, with a black scarf thing. It was the other way round from the painting.'

'As if the colours had been reversed? As if you were seeing... a kind of negative?' Sam was getting interested, in spite of himself.

'Yes. I hadn't thought of that,' Magnus said humbly, 'that's exactly right'.

'And what did she do? Did she speak to you? Did she look at you at all?'

'No. Ghosts don't.'

'You've met one before then?'

'*Listen*, are you taking this seriously or not?' Magnus said to Sam, getting his courage back.

'Perhaps the people I should be talking to are the Colonel and Cousin M,' and he fell silent.

'Sorry... sorr*ee*.'

'Get to the end of the story, Mags, ' said Floss. 'Come on.'

'Well, that is the end. It looked as though she was frozen, in a picture, and sort of being rolled across the room, except that she'd got these little white gloves and she kept twisting them into a ball. Oh and I couldn't see her feet at all, or the bottom part of her dress, and that's because I was seeing her nearly four hundred years ago, when the floor of the room was much lower. Do you remember? Colonel Stickley said it had been raised.'

'Wow!' said Sam, 'that's right. He did.' The scientific nature of this explanation appealed to him, but first you had to believe that there *were* ghosts.

'Well, what are we going to do about what you've seen, Mags?' Floss asked him. She didn't quite know what she thought. He had sounded utterly convincing but he obviously had a powerful imagination and it was just possible he'd dreamed the whole thing about coming downstairs last night. Dreams were sometimes so vivid it was hard to believe you were not awake, when you were in the middle of them. It was harder to explain what he had seen in the Council Chamber and the details were so precise. She found them convincing.

'I'm going to write down absolutely everything that's happened so far,' he said, 'in a notebook. I brought one. And then... well, I'd like to talk to Colonel Stickley.'

'D'you want us all to talk to him?'

'I don't know, yet. Let me think about it.'

'Sooner you than me,' Sam grunted, rolling his modesty screen into position so he could put on his swimming trunks.

But Floss whispered, 'We're on your side, Mags.'

'*Are* you?' he said. 'But Sam doesn't seem to believe me. What does "being on my side" mean?'

'It means,' Floss answered slowly, 'that I – that we – er, love you, and believe in you, even if we're not sure yet about the ghosts.'

Magnus turned pink. But she suspected he was pleased.

Sam emerged wearing a pair of old shorts with his swimming trunks underneath. 'Let's go and find Maude,' he said, 'and ask her about the pool. It's so stuffy up here. I want a swim.'

The round turret room was retaining the heat quite amazingly. Magnus ran his eyes up and down the freshly-painted walls. 'There are some terrible cracks here,' he said. 'Have you noticed them? There are some on the landings as well. I expect they run down through all the rooms. Do you think Colonel Stickley knows about them?'

Sam shrugged. 'Dunno. Are they important? The place isn't going to fall down, is it, after eight hundred years?'

'Is it really that old?' said Floss.

'Parts of it are... what on earth are you doing, Mags?'

Magnus had produced a large strip of sticking plaster and was laying it carefully across one of the biggest cracks, just inside the fireplace. 'You have to allow a bit of give,' he said. 'It's called a tell-tale.'

'A what?'

'It tells you if the walls are moving apart. Builders do it a lot. We must check this for movement every day. If the plaster gets tighter then the crack is widening.'

'I see. And what are we going to do if the walls fall down?' Sam said sarcastically.

'They won't. It takes years, usually. I think it's all the hot summers we've had. The ground that this tower is built on must have dried out, and shrunk.'

'I'm off,' said Sam impatiently. It was so hot. 'You two can do what you like. And if I see Colonel Stickley I'm going to tell him that we're occupying a hard hat area. I'll leave the ghost bits to you, Mags.'

'Listen, don't be mean to him,' Floss whispered, catching him up as he made his way down the spiral staircase.

'Well I can't cope. I'd no idea he could be so, so *weird*. First it's ghosts that step out of picture frames, then it's cracks in the walls and bits of plaster. Nothing feels very normal round here.'

'That's because it's not,' Magnus informed him in a perfectly matter-of-fact voice. He had obviously heard every word.

V

In the walled garden Maude was having trouble with her sprinkler, and also with Arthur. She was trying to sow some seeds from a packet, but as soon as she had patted the earth back over her carefully-made drills, the cat dug them up again. Then he lay down in them, purring, and began to chew the empty seed packets which, impaled on twigs, marked where everything had been planted. 'This is *hopeless*,' she said in exasperation, chasing him off. 'He thinks he's a dog. I've never known a cat chew things. He's in absolute disgrace with Colonel Stickley; he keeps chewing up *The Times*.' She looked at the sprinkler which was dribbling feebly out of only half its holes. 'And look at that. Do you think he's chewed that up too?'

Sam inspected the sprinkler and noticed that the hosepipe attached to it was kinked up in several places. As soon as he straightened it out the water wooshed out with terrific force, soaking them all. Nobody minded getting wet, it was so warm, but

Arthur fled to a safe viewing point on top of a rose arch.

Sam was thinking how peculiar it was that Cousin M, who was a professional gardener and who'd written books on the subject, hadn't noticed all those knots in the hosepipe. Gardeners were usually such practical people.

But then she said, 'It's really most odd, getting all those kinks in the pipe. No wonder the sprinkler was bunged up. Thank you, dear. That was such a help.' In spite of himself, and although he was determined not to get obsessed like Magnus, or to start seeing things where there was probably nothing to see, Sam couldn't help thinking of Cousin M's flower arrangement in the turret room fireplace, and of how the white petals had been torn to pieces. If there really were some ghostly women around then they had a grudge against people.

'It seems ridiculous to have sprinklers on all the time,' Cousin Maude went on. 'They banned sprinklers and hosepipes last year, and they'll be banning them again if we don't get some rain soon. Life would be a lot easier for me if we concreted this whole place over. Perish the thought.'

'But it's *gorgeous*, Cousin M,' said Floss, looking round at the ancient kitchen garden with its rusty brick walls smothered in every conceivable thing that grew. There were not only roses and honeysuckles, but vines and serious-looking fruit trees, their branches trained into intricate patterns along wires fixed into the masonry. There were orderly rows of vegetables and there were flowerbeds, there was a sundial and a pond with a fountain and, right in the middle, there was a maze with fat little box hedges. It was so small you got to the middle in no time and, as all the children were taller than the hedges, there was no danger of getting lost. They were soon right in the centre of it, where they found an ancient statue of a little child. It was made of some greenish metal, its ridged curls covered with bird-droppings, a child with gently-folded hands that stared rather sadly into another small pool, covered with waterlily leaves.

Cousin M was obviously pleased that Floss approved of her garden, but she didn't seem to want anybody lingering by the statue. 'Colonel Stickley doesn't really like people coming here,' she said apologetically, leading them out of the maze. 'It's rather a special place to him, I mean where the statue is. He likes to sit there and smoke his pipe.'

'Why is it special?' asked Magnus.

Cousin M paused. 'Well, he did have a wife,' she said, 'but she died a long time ago. There is a son, David – oh, he'll be at least forty by now, though I still think of him as a young boy. I can see him now, playing in this garden.'

Magnus said sharply, 'Where is he? You said *is* not *was*.' Sam and Floss exchanged looks. He was in his detective mood again, firing questions at everybody.

But the odd, abrupt manner which so irritated them didn't seem to offend Cousin M. She said, 'Yes, dear, I did. He's a very clever man, he speaks a lot of languages. He worked abroad for a newspaper and he was captured some years ago by a group of terrorists – two of them were captured. They'd insisted on entering a no-go area, to try and get some photographs. It's the usual story I'm afraid. They just disappeared. He *is* alive – well, he was three years ago. But his father hasn't heard anything about him since then, when the man they captured at the same time was released. It's really terrible for my cousin, not knowing what has become of his only child.'

The three of them looked very grave and no-one knew what to say. Then Floss spoke. 'He must think it's part of the curse,' she said, 'and why nothing's gone right here for years and years. Does it really go back to that horrible-looking monk, that – what was he called?'

'Burst Belly,' Magnus informed her.

'I don't think so, dear,' Cousin M said calmly. 'Families do have runs of bad luck and some have very tragic histories, but as for curses, well, I don't believe in that sort of thing at all.' She bent down and began to attack a clump of weeds that were growing up vigorously in the middle of a seed drill. 'Now, you could say *this* was a curse, just look at those roots!'

'You're like me,' Sam told her, squatting down in the flowerbed and helping her pull them out.

'Am I really, dear? That's very encouraging. How, exactly?'

'Well, you're practical and you don't seem to believe old wives' tales.'

Cousin M grinned. 'Even though I'm a bit of an old wife myself?'

'I didn't mean that,' Sam began, feeling confused. 'I just meant that I get the feeling you wouldn't take Magnus's theories about the Abbey very seriously.'

Cousin Maude straightened up. 'Ouch! That's my back. I really *must* remember to get up more slowly, doctor's orders.' She shook the earth off her trowel then looked at Magnus. 'What are these "theories" of yours about the Abbey, dear? I don't think I've heard about them.'

Magnus opened his mouth but Sam got in first. Magnus's rather slow and pedantic manner of speaking, when he was really gripped by something, got on his nerves. 'He thinks the Abbey might be haunted and that that's why people don't book conferences here any more, or use the sports centre. Have *you* seen anything, Cousin M?'

She looked him straight in the eyes. Then she

looked equally keenly at Magnus and Floss. Silence had fallen on the old garden. They were all waiting for her to speak.

'No, dears, I haven't, not ever. I've not lived in the Abbey all that long, I only came back here two years ago. Cecil didn't want to lose the place and he needed a business partner. I had some money to invest and I wanted to get my hands on another garden. So, well, here I am. I don't really understand why people have stopped coming here. It's a perfect sort of place, I think.'

'Who *does* know about the Abbey, then?' demanded Magnus. 'Colonel Stickley doesn't seem to want to talk about it, or to show us things. But I suspect he *does* think there are ghosts around, he's like me.'

'Really? What do you mean by that, dear?'

'Well, in some people,' Magnus began in the high-pitched, detective voice that was becoming familiar to them, 'the veil between this world and the spirit world is very, very thin. Those are the people who see things.'

'Or think they do,' Sam muttered.

"I see. That's very well put. I think I'm not one of those people, Magnus. My feet are very firmly planted on the earth, you could say. I'm not a person who "sees things", or picks up special atmospheres.'

'I just wish somebody would take me seriously,' Magnus said. His voice had become rather petulant and complaining but, even as the words came out, he felt ashamed of himself. The Colonel's only son, David, who would have inherited the Abbey, was missing, presumed dead. That in itself was a truly terrible thing. No wonder he wandered about at night and brooded by the fire. The missing son felt like a curse in itself; you didn't need ghosts as well.

'Does Wilf know anything?' asked Floss. The small lean-looking man frying bacon in his khaki shorts had seemed quite friendly.

'I don't know what Wilf knows,' Maude told her. 'But he's a real no-nonsense type. I wouldn't think he'd have much time for spooks. He was in the war, with the Colonel. He was his batman.'

Sam, visualising Batman and Robin flying off on some dangerous mission, smiled to himself, not able to square this picture with Wilf and the Colonel.

Cousin Maude saw the smile. 'Oh, it just means he was his *aide*,' she explained. 'He did the practical things, when they were on military manoeuvres. Wilf's my cousin's best friend – but I'm not sure how much he knows about the Abbey.'

She stared across the vegetable plot, spotted more unofficial greenery, frowned and prepared to do battle. 'Japanese Knot Weed… whatever next? It's *lethal*!' Then, as she picked up her trowel again, her face suddenly cleared. 'There *is* somebody who knows a lot about the Abbey,' she said 'but I'm not sure. I imagine you wouldn't really want to go visiting the sick.'

'Who is it?' asked Floss.

'Everybody calls her Miss Adeline,' explained Cousin M. 'She's over ninety, but she's certainly in her right mind. She's got a wonderful memory and she's as sharp as a needle. She's very frail though, and she's going blind. She loves having visitors and she's quite a talker, if she's got someone who'll listen. I call in most days, but of course it's only boring old me. She'd love it if someone young were to drop by, I know she would. She was born in the Abbey and she's never lived anywhere else.'

'Where's her house?' asked Magnus. This ancient lady sounded the most promising thing so far. He felt very warm towards Cousin M. She may not believe in ghosts but she'd just given him the opportunity to do some serious research.

'It's the Lodge by the front gates. You passed it last night, in the dark. If you'd like to go I'll make her up a few goodies. She has those rather boring meals in tins delivered most days. I think a bit of home cooking wouldn't go amiss. Would you like to go after lunch? I've got quite a bit more to do here.'

'"Luncheon is at twelve-thirty",' quoted Magnus, in a flat voice. '"It will be a light repast."' Maude stared at him quizzically. Did he have a very subtle sense of humour or was he poking sly fun at Colonel Stickley?

'Wilf said it was only going to be cheese-and-pickle sandwiches,' Sam explained solidly. Then he added, 'I'm going to see if I can get into the swimming pool first. I'm melting.'

They found the pool quite near the front gates, near Miss Adeline's house, which turned out to be a beautiful old cottage with brick and flint walls, a sagging roof of crumbling red tiles and a messy, tangled garden. Cousin Maude no doubt would have whipped out her secateurs and set it to rights in no time but Sam, who had some experience of old ladies, worked out that this Miss Adeline would have her own views. Not that he intended to come visiting. He had other plans.

The old cottage presented a sharp contrast to the swimming pool building which resembled a mini aircraft hangar and was built of ugly yellow brick. 'It's a good thing most of it's hidden under the trees,' said Floss. 'How could Colonel Stickley have put up such a monstrosity? It's hideous.'

'I expect he was saving money,' Sam said.

The main door of the building was open and admitted them into a cool tiled entrance hall filled with bedraggled-looking pot plants. The windows were smeary, there was a stale, musty smell and a definite feeling that nobody used the place much. but it *was* a swimming pool, and it was a large one, a serious rectangular pool, not silly, in the shape of a piano or a whale, and through glazed inner doors they could see gently moving waters of a bright mediterranean blue. There was nobody swimming, it was all theirs. Sam's heart rose. He adored being the first in. 'Let's go,' he said.

But when he pressed the handle down he found that the inner door was firmly locked. He rattled it in frustration yelling 'Damn! This was the only thing I wanted, and now it's locked!'

Floss tried the door too, and banged on the glass. She quite wanted a swim herself. She'd improved recently and she reckoned her front crawl might be faster than Sam's.

'No good trying to break the door down,' Magnus told them sententiously. Secretly, he was much relieved. He'd been dreading this moment, being exposed as a poor swimmer in front of the others. He'd been planning to slip down to the pool on his own some time, and practise in secret. 'Wilf probably knows about the pool,' he said. 'Why don't you ask him when it's open?'

'I'm going to. I'm going to do it right now,' Sam answered, giving the locked door a final kick before turning away.

'Wait for me,' Floss said. 'Come on, Mags.'

Magnus watched them running off down the drive. Then something made him turn and look back, some physical thing, some force that seemed to be drawing him like a magnet towards the bright blue water which shimmered at him through the locked glazed doors. And she was there again, the woman in the white dress, moving over the surface of the bright blue panelled water, in a kind of soft-edged haze.

This time Magnus found that he wanted to hold his ground. He felt no fear. If asked why, he would have answered that there was nothing to be afraid of, because he could clearly see the woman's face. This was because the apparition was scarcely moving, rather hovering over the pool, anxiously twisting the little white gloves in her thin fingers, reducing them to a crumpled ball. And the face was not a face to instil terror.

It was certainly the face of the portrait in the great hall and, like the painting, it was proud and haughty. But round the mouth there was something else, less of certainty, more of regret. Some grievous memory was softening what he'd thought was a harsh face. The apparition's eyes, as in the painting, were blue, a colour he'd always thought of as hard and cold. But now, momentarily, the woman stopped moving, turned her head and looked at him and he saw two tears roll slowly down her cheeks.

He cried out. 'Speak to me.' But the apparition merely stared down at him, taking in, he thought, his height and age, registering the fact that she was looking at a mere child who could be no use to her, she who had walked with a queen.

Then the figure opened its mouth but Magnus could hear nothing through the thick glass criss-crossed with its web of fine wires. In desperation he hammered on the window. 'Come to me!' he cried 'Oh, come to me! Tell me why you are not at peace in this world,' strange words that did not feel like his own, words that had been given him to speak, by another being.

At once the figure vanished and the blue water surged up in a great wave and splashed over the edges of the swimming pool. Magnus felt weak, he had to clutch on to the edge of the window in the door to stop himself sagging down. He felt bitterly cold, great goose pimples stood out all over his arms and legs and his teeth were chattering. He took one last desperate look through the swimming pool door to see if the vision had really gone away, but found he could not see through because the glass in the windows was skinned with ice.

He walked very slowly after the others. He wouldn't tell them yet. He believed a very important pattern might be forming, a pattern that involved them all. But to understand what it all meant they would have to be patient, like bird-watchers sitting quietly in their hides or anglers waiting for the fish to bite. The most significant thing about what had just happened was that for the first time when the ghostly woman had been present he hadn't felt afraid, and that she had communicated with him – or at least there had been the beginnings of a communication. His banging on the glass, which he regretted now, had frightened her away and that meant she was not locked in her own time, as he had understood from Father Godless was the usual way of ghosts. For a few minutes in the swimming pool building she had stepped from her time into his, perhaps because she needed the modern people in the Abbey. Or could it be that she just needed Magnus?

They found Wilf making sandwiches in the buttery. He knew all about the costs of the day-to-day running of the Abbey, and he was able to explain about the swimming pool.

'It costs a lot to run, a pool like that,' he said. 'It's the maintenance. And with nobody coming on these courses any more there's no point in keeping it open, not all the time. But the Colonel goes in every day, briefly – swimming's good for his injury, stops him stiffening up. And your Aunt Maude insists—'

'*Cousin* Maude,' said Magnus.

'The lady insists on letting folk from the village come, now and again. The nearest public pool is in High Wycombe and they don't all have transport. The Colonel's not keen of course, but he can only stay on here because of her money, so he's got to give way on some things.'

'Did he really not want us to come here, Wilf?'

asked Magnus. 'Doesn't he like children?' He felt very emotional. Sam and Floss's parents had given him a lot of love since he'd come to live with them and although he could not forget what had happened in his own family, and still dreamed terrible dreams about it, the way this new family treated him seemed to be healing something inside him, healing it with their love. Colonel Stickley had been quite kind to him, when they'd been on their own in the middle of the night, but most of the time he was grumpy and irritable. Magnus found it very hard to trust him and he very much wanted to.

Wilf, seeing tears in his eyes, patted him on the shoulder. 'No, lad, he doesn't dislike young people, not at all. But he has this sadness to cope with, about his son.'

'The one who's missing? Cousin M told us,' Floss explained.

Sam said, 'Do you think he's dead, Wilf?'

The little man paused, then let out a big sigh. 'It seems pretty likely, to me.' He slapped big chunks of chicken between slices of bread, sprinkling on lemon juice and a dash of curry powder, and feeding scraps to Arthur who was sitting hopefully under the table. 'About this swimming lark,' he said. 'Your only chance is the early morning.'

'What time?' asked Sam suspiciously. He liked lying-in during the holidays; he was hopeless at getting up early.

'Six-ish. Or you could go when the village people swim. I'll find out what's happening this week.'

'What about the multi-gym?' Sam asked next. He'd seen, again through locked glazed doors, glimpses of the most brilliant sports equipment, all laid out in a sports hall; tread-mills, cycling machines, rowing machines – thousands of pounds worth of stuff all sitting there unused. And they had inspected the tennis courts too. They were marvellous, miles better than the ones they played on at school. Yet these also were firmly padlocked and notices everywhere said 'Temporarily Out of Use'.

Wilf said, 'Listen, I'll tell you what I know, though it's not very much. And when I've told you, do you think you could let it drop and concentrate on your holiday? There's plenty to do here. You can go on the river and I'll try to get permission about the swimming, and there are some great walks round here – don't keep asking all these questions though; it doesn't help anybody.'

'But what *do* you know?' asked Magnus persistently. Grown-ups were so good at sliding off the point.

Wilf covered his plates of sandwiches carefully with plastic film, sat down and took Arthur on to his lap, almost like a bit of protection against these over-inquisitive children. He said, 'The colonel and I have been together since the war. We were very young men when it ended. We... a lot happened to us. He won medals. He's a brave man – and a *good* man,' he added quite fiercely. 'Anyhow, I had no family much so I stuck with the Colonel. He got married but they didn't send me packing, and I helped, when his young wife was so ill, and then died. David, his son, was only little. We brought him up together.'

'So you must miss him too?' Magnus observed, his driving need to know everything getting the better of his tact.

Wilf pulled at Arthur's ears, drawing out of him big, rapturous purrs. 'Yes, Magnus. I miss him. He'd have liked this cat. He always wanted to be a vet.

'The Colonel inherited the Abbey, eventually, from another branch of his family that had nobody else to leave it to. He was just a second cousin of a lady whose two sons had both been killed in the Second World War, killed in two separate battles. Hard to believe, isn't it? There was quite a bit of money too. So he thought he'd turn it into a place where young people could come, to do sport really seriously, in beautiful surroundings. He felt it was a kind of memorial to those two dead boys. Of course, people had to pay, but a lot of them got grants, and he never turned people away. He started with tennis and had all the courts laid out, then later, he added the swimming pool and the multi-gym. The very best people came to coach the young folk and it became quite famous, this place; they were queueing up to get on the courses. And then—'

He stopped and his lean brown body seemed to go rigid, quite suddenly. Arthur jumped off his knee and went to sit under the table again where he engaged in vigorous washing.

'Then *what*?'

Wilf hesitated. 'People started making complaints. It began with the adults, not the kids. First some of the top tennis coaches upped and left, just abandoned the young people in the middle of their training. Well, their parents had paid out a lot of money for them to come, some of the coaches were ex-Wimbledon. There was a lot of nasty business, about money. The Colonel had to go to court.'

'But that doesn't seem bad enough to close the place down,' Sam said. 'Not that on its own.'

'It wasn't, not at first. But it's funny, word gets round. Places get bad reputations and people start to avoid them, and go elsewhere – especially when children are involved. Anyhow, the Colonel weathered the court case and got new coaches. But then, the kids themselves started to complain.'

'What about?'

Wilf looked uneasy. 'They just… didn't like staying here, particularly in the turret rooms, where most of the dormitories are. They kept asking to be moved. So the Colonel brought in some portakabins. You've seen them, I expect, they're down behind the tennis courts. Nothing spooky about a portakabin, for heaven's sake.'

'*What* was spooky?' said Magnus. They were at last getting to the point.

'Just let me finish, Magnus,' Wilf said patiently.

'The crunch came when a girl had an accident. She was found in the garden, very early one morning, at the foot of the turret block. She had two broken legs and she'd injured her back. She made a full recovery, as it happened, but she *could* have broken her neck. Her father was quite a well-known politician. There was an enormous fuss and the Colonel – typical of him, I must say – just closed down the whole operation, while they conducted an enquiry.'

'And what did the enquiry prove?' said Sam. He dimly remembered such a case, on the television news.

'Nothing really. They could have just been larking about in the dormitories, or drinking. I don't know. But the Colonel was blamed and somehow, well, it broke his spirit. He never re-opened the Abbey as a sports centre. He's tried to get big companies to hold their conferences here, but people just don't book. And all because of that silly girl who was probably a bit drunk. I'm telling you, I could wring her neck!'

'But why do you think she jumped out of the

window, Wilf?' Magnus wanted to know.

'I haven't a clue, and that's the truth. When it happened they were all asleep in bed. The coaches had gone the rounds and all was well. Any larking about was long since over for the night. Now I've told you what I know. The best thing you can do for the Colonel, and for Miss Maude, is to keep mum, enjoy the Abbey and not jump out of any windows. Got it?'

'We couldn't anyway,' Magnus explained solemnly. 'We've got bars in our room.'

'That's right,' said Wilf. 'They barred all the windows after the accident but it didn't make any difference. People still didn't sign up for the courses.'

'Why on earth did they put us in one of the turret rooms, Wilf?' Sam asked.

He grinned. 'Well they nearly didn't, they had a real ding-dong about it, the Colonel and your cousin. He wanted you to have a portakabin but she said no, too damp and smelly and I must say I agree – not that I said anything, mind you. She said the turret rooms were always warmer than anywhere else, which is true, and she wanted you to have the very nicest of all, which you've got, and if there was any larking about which of course she knew there wouldn't be, because she knew you were perfect children, every flipping window in the place more or less is barred now. Also, of course... 'but here his voice died away. 'Oh never

mind. Here, Arthur, fancy a bit of bacon old chap?'

Magnus grabbed his arm feverishly. 'Also *what*?' Why, oh why, did grown-ups have this infuriating habit of drying up at the most crucial moment?

'*Also*,' said Wilf, shaking Magnus off quite vigorously, 'the two of them had a basic disagreement. In a nutshell, the Colonel has this notion that the Abbey is haunted at certain times by the ghost of Lady Alice Neale, the woman in the portrait, and your cousin thinks it's a load of poppycock. I reckon she wanted to show him just how much credence she placed in the things people say by putting you in the turret. *So*... seen anything yet? Who are you putting your money on, the Colonel or your Cousin Maude?' And he grinned at them. It was pretty obvious whose side he was on.

Magnus answered for them all. He clearly did not want to divulge anything of his private 'sightings' to Wilf, not at that moment. 'We need to talk about it,' he said crisply, 'we all have... rather different views at the moment.'

'"Curiouser and curiouser",' Floss muttered as they went outside and started walking towards the river. She was thinking, not of the Lady Neale, but of another, less formidable Alice.

VI

'I'm not coming to see this old lady,' Sam said when they were back in the turret room. 'It sounds a bit too like – well, I'm just not coming.' He spoke very firmly; his mind was obviously made up.

'But why not?' asked Magnus. 'She knows all the history.'

Sam didn't reply, merely kicked open his suitcase to get a fresh T-shirt. He was dripping with sweat.

Floss led Magnus over to the window and whispered, letting her words float out over the gardens. 'I think it's because of our Aunt Helen,' she explained, 'well, our Great Aunt. Sam's her godson and she's had a stroke. He doesn't like going to visit her any more. It's too sad for him. OK?'

'OK,' Magnus said, unquestioningly. Then, to her surprise, he walked rather nervously up to Sam's divan and gave him a little pat. 'They're horrible, strokes,' he said, in a very grown-up voice. 'My friend Father Godless had one too. He dribbles now.'

Sam stared at him, not comprehending, then, suspiciously, at Floss. Then he turned his back, stripped off his T-shirt and pulled on a fresh one. 'I suppose the tennis whizz-kids were always changing their things,' he said, 'like they do at Wimbledon. Do you think it was *this* window that stupid girl jumped out of?' And he examined the metal bars. 'I can't tell how old these are, but they've been freshly painted.'

Magnus came and inspected the bars too. Then he stuck his head out of the window, manoeuvring his small neat ears past the metal struts, sideways, so he could see the ground. 'It's an awfully long way down,' he said. 'It's a miracle she wasn't killed.'

Floss said, peering out too, 'But do you think she *did* jump? Might she have been pushed – like Humpty Dumpty? "Humpty Dumpty was pushed", that's what people are saying now. In other words, he didn't fall off the wall by accident.'

Sam and Magnus laughed, but not for very long. 'Are you saying somebody tried to murder her?' Sam said.

'I don't know. But if she was a famous politician's daughter it could have been a government plot.'

'Perhaps your Miss Adeline will tell you more,'

Sam muttered, foraging in his case for fresh socks. He'd decided his feet were smelly.

Floss said rather peevishly, 'She's not "my" Miss Adeline. Sam, won't you change your mind, and come with us? She's OK, "sharp as a needle" Cousin M said.'

'No. I'm going to look round the village. Wilf's lending me his bike. There's a big memorial to the Neale family in the church. That's *real* history.'

'Have it your own way,' Floss said, and went off. But Magnus, who was privately getting more and more taken up with the history of the Abbey, seemed to approve of this division of labour. 'We could report back here later this afternoon,' he said, 'and we can pool our ideas.'

'Report on what, Mags?' Floss asked. 'We're only taking an old lady a few home-made cakes.'

'You know it's more than that,' he said, quite frostily, 'and I think it's rather serious. I'm wondering if we ought to move out of this room. They could put us in one of those portakabins.'

Floss stared at him. 'What do you mean... that somebody might try to attack us, or something?'

'Well, why not? Somebody wrecked Maude's flowers while we were asleep.'

'It was the *cat*, Mags,' Sam said in exasperation. 'Keep calm, can't you, and stop imagining things. I'm off. See you later.'

'OK. How about meeting in the walled garden at five o'clock?' suggested Floss. She giggled.

'We could have – what does the Colonel call it – a "light repast"?'

Cousin M had put together a pretty basket of goodies for Miss Adeline: a brown loaf, still warm, some scones, two fresh eggs laid by Eunice, an eccentric brown hen that followed her round the gardens, and a posy of flowers. 'Tell her that I'll call in later, to boil her a tea-time egg, if she'd like,' she said, watching them crunch off along the gravelled drive towards the Lodge.

Before they were half-way there, Sam trundled past on an ancient black bicycle. 'See you,' he said, then he called back cheekily, 'I'm off to dig up some *proper* history.'

'Why is he like that?' Magnus asked Floss.

'Like what?'

'So… so against things, so… sceptical,' he added, pleased to have found the correct word.

'I think he's just nervous. Sam doesn't like things he can't understand. He's very practical.'

Soon they were standing in front of a dark green door and lifting a knocker of polished brass. The door was freshly painted and the knocker gleamed. There were tubs of sweet-smelling flowers on the doorstep, in spite of the chaos of the overgrown garden that surrounded the cottage. It all looked cared-for. Floss wondered if Cousin M had put the tubs there, wanting the old lady to smell some flowers, even if she could not see them very well.

They lifted the knocker three times but nobody came. Then they listened, their ears close to the door, in case the old woman should be shuffling along to open it, but they could hear nothing.

'She's out,' Magnus concluded, disappointed and finding his mouth was watering at the smell of the new loaf and the scones. 'What do we do now?'

Then, 'No, she's not out, she's just very slow,' said a clear, high voice, and the green door was pulled inwards. 'It's Magnus, Florence and Samuel, isn't it?' she paused. 'But there are only two of you.' She had stretched out her hands and was feeling towards them, touching, first their arms and shoulders, then their faces. She was tiny and her body was bent almost double, and she peered up at them through rheumy blue eyes. 'I don't see too well, but there *are* only the two of you. I'm right, aren't I?'

'Yes,' said Floss. 'Sam – Samuel, my brother, couldn't come today. Cousin Maude sent you these things.' And she held the basket out.

'Well, come along to my drawing room,' said the old lady, closing the door. Her voice was not exactly bossy, but it was firm. She seemed used to being obeyed and she hadn't said please. Nor had she said thank you for the basket of good things. Magnus and Floss followed behind her very slowly because she could only creep along, down a cool narrow hall tiled in black and white diamonds, a hall hung with paintings which they were dying to inspect. They were smaller than the ones in the Abbey but they looked equally ancient and many were of people in Elizabethan dress.

'Drawing room' sounded extremely grand, but the room to which Miss Adeline led them was small and low-ceilinged, beamed with a great inglenook fireplace and crammed in every corner with delicate old furniture, all carefully polished. They could smell beeswax and lavender. On the floor were faded, beautiful rugs and the shelves and windowsills were crowded with pieces of painted porcelain, with gilded plates on special stands and fragile cups and saucers. There was a glass-fronted cabinet full of silver.

Looking at everything, at the dark cottage room stuffed full of valuable artefacts that seemed to belong to a rather grander life, at a little parlour which the old lady had called a 'drawing room', Floss remembered what Cousin Maude had told her about Miss Adeline, when she was packing the goody basket. She didn't live on the Abbey estate because the Colonel felt sorry for her or because her family had been servants. Her family had owned it all, once. But, like so many other branches of it, they had been obliged to let it pass out of their hands because there had been nobody left to inherit. In her case, it should have gone to a brother, but he had been killed in the First World War. It was exactly as Colonel Stickley had told them. No family survived intact long enough to inherit and pass it on to their children, and to their children's children. The lovely things in the cottage must have been in the Abbey once. Floss felt sad when she looked at them.

'Sit down,' said Miss Adeline. 'I thought we might take tea in about an hour.' A table by the fireplace was already set out, with four cups and saucers and four plates, brown bread and butter and a cake, and jam in a glass jar. 'Would you remove Samuel's cup and saucer for me?' she said, 'as he is not coming.' Floss decided that she was more disappointed than annoyed. He really should have come. Old people who lived alone set great store by visits and they didn't like changes of plan.

She said, settling herself in a wing chair with a high back, 'Maude tells me you are interested in the history of the Abbey, and that you've been asking her a lot of questions she can't answer. Why, may I ask? Why all these questions? The young people usually come here to play tennis, or to swim.'

Floss and Magnus exchanged looks, then they both looked rather sheepishly at the old lady who had leaned forward intently to listen, her tiny claw hands bunched together in her lap. A narrow shaft of sunlight filtered through a window on to her fine white hair and her string of small seed pearls, and on the red-purple Paisley scarf knotted round her neck. She was rather sharp-featured and very thin but Floss decided that she must once have been rather beautiful. She had a regal air, she was somebody obviously used to giving orders. She hadn't been a servant girl, washing floors up at the Big House, but a child of the family.

'Because,' Magnus began courageously, in a firm voice, 'we think there is something wrong here.'

Miss Adeline did not react nor seem put out in any way. She merely said, 'I take it you have seen the Lady Alice Neale?'

'Yes,' said Magnus. 'Well, I've seen something. And the other two have heard her crying – that is, Floss has.'

'Samuel heard her as well,' Floss added.

The old lady leaned back against the worn green chair and closed her eyes. 'So she is abroad again,' she murmured. 'It's the usual pattern. The young come, and she walks. Only when the Abbey is thoroughly emptied of its young will she leave it in peace. Unless—'

'Unless *what*?' Magnus said urgently. 'What needs to happen?'

Miss Adeline looked at him blankly. She seemed quite unaware that she had been speaking her thoughts aloud. 'Has she come out of her frame?' she said. 'Is that what you are telling me?'

'Yes, I am.' She was so very calm and matter-of-fact about it that Magnus was encouraged to be matter-of-fact too. 'Last night something definitely woke me up, a woman, sighing and weeping. I followed the sound and when I got to the Great Hall, where all the pictures are, I saw the frame, where the portrait should have been, and it was blank.'

'What else did you see?'

'Nothing. The Colonel took me back to bed. He was awfully cross.'

'Where is bed?' enquired Miss Adeline.

'In the turret. On the top floor.'

The old lady sucked in her lips. 'Where that silly girl fell from the window.'

'They've put bars up now,' Floss explained.

'There were always bars, my dear, it was a night nursery. I slept in it myself, with my brother Maurice. Magnus, bring me the silver photograph frame from the walnut bookcase,' she said.

Magnus did so and laid it carefully between her stiff, waiting fingers. The old lady brought it close to her face, then, to their amazement, she gave it a gentle kiss. 'My lovely brother,' she said. 'He was killed in the Battle of the Somme. He was eighteen years old, cannon fodder. It was a war fought by children.'

Silence filled the room like something totally solid. Floss wanted to reach out and touch the old lady who sat clutching the photograph, as fragile, suddenly, as her delicate china cups. She said, 'We are sorry, Miss Adeline.'

'Thank you, Florence. At my age, you live mainly with ghosts. There's nobody much else left.'

Then she said, in a firmer voice, 'Has she visited you in the turret room?'

'Yes,' said Magnus, 'And she seems angry. For example, Cousin Maude put some flowers in there for us, and they were wrecked.'

'What kind of flowers?'

'I'm not sure. Could they have been peonies? They looked a bit like roses, but they had no smell.'

'Go into the hall, Magnus,' she ordered. 'On your left, by the grandfather clock, you'll see a small picture. Bring it to us, please.'

Magnus set off again to find the picture. It all felt so strange to Floss and yet, somehow, right, almost inevitable, Magnus taking these orders from the half-blind old lady, unquestioning, with the obvious feeling that all of it was meant to be. She did not mind at all sitting quietly by. And she was glad Sam had gone to the village. She felt there might be a purpose in that, too.

The picture Magnus unhooked carefully from the wall was identical to the one he had seen in the Great Hall in the Abbey – the head of a small pretty-looking boy with a white flower between his fingers. He said, placing it carefully in her lap,

'It's the same one as in the Abbey, isn't it? I asked Colonel Stickley about it.'

'This is the *original*,' said Miss Adeline, moving her fingers across the surface of the painting, as if they could perform the act of seeing for her useless eyes. 'The one in the Abbey is a copy. Now the fact that the painting was copied indicates to me that this young boy was important. But nobody knows who he was. What did the Colonel tell you, Magnus?'

"That he might have been a son of Lady Alice, but that nobody really knows. He's not in the parish records or anything.'

'Correct,' said Miss Adeline crisply, but she seemed to Floss to be definitely thawing, and very excited at having a story of her own to tell, and two eager children to tell it to. 'The next thing you need to know – just to keep the facts straight – is that these white flowers are one of our clues. They are not peonies, by the way, peonies don't flower so early in the year, and they're bigger blooms. They're an old-fashioned English flower, quite rare. Oh, it's an impossible Latin name. I did know it once. Let me try and remember...' She screwed up her face in a great effort of concentration.

Magnus said impatiently, 'It doesn't matter about the name. Why are the flowers important?'

'Because the Lady Alice Neale is always distressed by them. Did Maude Cousin tell you about the eve of the conference?'

'No,' Floss and Magnus said in chorus.

'Well, about this time last year, an international company booked the Abbey for a conference. It was great news for the Colonel. It meant a lot of money – he'd been having a very difficult time. Well, the evening it began, they left their business papers in the Great Hall which had been set out as the conference room. Maude had put floral arrangements on each of the tables and she'd used the peony flowers, because the garden was full of them. When they'd all gone to dine in the Solar – the lower dining room with the river view, you'll have seen it perhaps – the Great Hall was locked up for the night. They'd left their official papers there and one or two had left their briefcases, ready for the morning session. When Wilf unlocked the door next morning, at about eight-thirty, somebody had been in there, and caused havoc. Two of the briefcases had been cut into pieces and all the official papers had been torn up.'

'And what about the peony flowers?' said Magnus.

'Every single arrangement had been thrown to the ground and the vases smashed to smithereens and —'

But Floss, who had been silent until now, interrupted. 'And the flowers had been ripped off their stems and pulled to pieces, petal by petal. Is that what had happened?'

Miss Adeline leaned forward and peered into

her face. 'My dear Florence, that is *exactly* right. How do you know so precisely?'

'Because that's what had been done to the flowers Cousin M put in the fireplace, in our dormitory.'

'Did you lock your door before retiring?'

'No. There isn't a key.'

'Well, the Great Hall was most definitely locked,' said Miss Adeline.

Magnus said thoughtfully, 'So the Lady Alice is sometimes violent?'

'Yes. She's a poltergeist, I suppose, an unquiet spirit who causes havoc.'

'But... but she's not mischievous, is she?' Magnus speculated, 'I mean, she doesn't indulge in mischief for its own sake?' He'd suddenly thought of all those loops and tangles in Maude's garden hose but decided not to mention them. It seemed trivial. 'It must be something to do with the boy, mustn't it, if he's the one holding the flower in the painting?'

'Does she not *want* to be reminded of him any more?' said Floss. 'Is that why she always destroys the flowers?'

'We don't know,' Miss Adeline said. 'Is it the boy that she weeps for and is he her son? There are so many questions here and nobody can ever answer them. They can only guess.'

Magnus said, 'Have you ever seen a ghost in the Abbey, Miss Adeline?'

She smiled at him and the smile made her look uncannily young. 'Well now, before we come to that, supposing you tell me what *you* have seen, first. I think that's fair. Age must have some privileges, you know, and I *am* going to give you afternoon tea.'

'I haven't seen anything,' Floss said, 'honestly I haven't. But, like Magnus said, I was woken up last night by the sound of somebody crying, and so was Sam – Samuel. We both felt very cold, all of a sudden. Sam put some socks on.'

'Yes. It is always cold when she walks,' Miss Adeline said thoughtfully. 'And you, Magnus, Magnus the Mighty One, what have you seen?'

Magnus flushed. 'Are you making fun of me?' he said, 'calling me that? You've got a funny name too, and I'm not making fun of you.' He didn't know what to make of this old lady. She was half-serious and half-mocking. Floss took in a sharp breath. Magnus could be so touchy and she didn't want Miss Adeline to take offence now, and send them away.

But the old lady inclined her head apologetically. 'I'm sorry. Only, Magnus is such a marvellous name. Please don't be cross. I'm so enjoying this visit.'

Magnus remained silent for a few seconds then, taking his time, he told her about the two apparitions, about the figure in white that had had no feet, which had glided across the Council

Chamber, and about what he thought he had seen through the window of the swimming pool, that fleeting shape which he was sure must have been the woman in distress because he had heard her voice again.

'You didn't tell me about that, Mags,' Floss said, rather hurt. Why had he kept such an important thing private?

'Thought you might laugh,' he muttered. 'Anyhow, I'm telling you now.'

Floss wanted to assure him that she would never, ever laugh at him, whatever he claimed to have seen. He was not fanciful and he was not a liar. Whatever Magnus told you, you believed. But Miss Adeline had started speaking again.

'What you saw in the Council Chamber,' she said, 'the ghost that appears to be cut off at the ankles, has been seen many times and people have written accounts of it. I expect Colonel Stickley told you that they raised the floor in 1850, so that is the explanation of why the woman appears to have no feet. And there are several people who claim to have seen the empty frame. Also—'

'But the woman in the Council Chamber wore white,' interrupted Magnus, 'a white dress with a black scarf thing, the other way round from the painting. Is it someone different?'

'We do not think so,' said Miss Adeline. 'It's just that, when she leaves her frame, the colours are always reversed, like a photographic negative.'

'That's what Sam said,' muttered Magnus, his respect for Floss's tough, rather impatient older brother increasing considerably.

'Lady Alice does not like to be moved,' said the old lady. 'We once let the painting go to London, to an exhibition. The night watchman, who sat up all night in the gallery where she'd been put on display, found the frame was empty, just like Magnus. He was terrified. He had to be transferred to another part of the building.'

'So there's only one ghost,' Magnus said. 'Well, that's something. Anyhow, that's all I've seen. What about you?'

She smiled her whimsical young-girl smile again. 'You're a persistent young man, Magnus, aren't you? Florence, please will you go through to the kitchen, the door's just behind you, and switch on the electric kettle. It always takes an age to boil. While it's heating up I'll tell you my side of things. But don't get excited. It's not much.'

'I'm not excited,' Magnus said, settling down on the squashy settee to listen. But his heart was thumping so loudly he thought Miss Adeline would surely hear.

VII

'Well, I was born here, as you know, ninety-three years ago this June, as was my brother Maurice, five years before me. If he had not been killed he would have inherited the Abbey and it would still be in my family. But it was not to be. They say that Burst Belly, that gross Black Canon, put a curse on the place when Henry the Eighth sent him away. Well, there are all kinds of curses, it seems to me. Hideous unjust wars that kill brave young men are curses, and that's happened twice this century and deprived the Abbey of its heirs. And now David Stickley is dead, or so we have to believe. Another war has taken another heir.

'You ask me what I have seen here. Well, I'm sorry to disappoint you but you seem to have seen and heard more in twenty-four hours than I have in a lifetime. The fact is, I've seen nothing. But I've heard too much from people I consider very sensible not to believe that the Abbey isn't haunted by an unhappy spirit. Whether that unhappiness has caused so many of the sad things in its history I wouldn't know. But of course, I think about that possibility. We all do, all of us who love this place.

'My only *personal* experience of the Lady Alice Neale happened when I was about your age, Florence. Maurice had already gone to fight in the Great War and wounded soldiers were sent here, to recover from their injuries. The solar and the adjoining rooms were turned into hospital wards and my mother organised nurses to look after them.'

She closed her eyes. 'There were some terrible injuries, my dears. The young men were very brave but sometimes they cried out in pain. As I say, I was only a young girl but the nurses let me help them. I learned to dress wounds and to make poultices, and the patients liked me to bathe their faces with lavender water. We used lavender from the garden, the bushes are still there.

'One night, I thought I heard one of them cry out in pain. I was sleeping in my mother's bed, in a little room off the solar. The noise didn't wake her but it woke me and I slipped out of the room to see who could be crying like that. I thought I might try to change a dressing myself, I was getting quite good at it – or perhaps the soldier just needed a cooling drink. It was very hot, rather like it is at the moment.

'When I got to the solar all the men were fast asleep. I went to each bed in turn, just to check, but they were all sleeping so deeply it seemed to me impossible that any of them could have made the crying noise. But I *had* heard it, it had woken me up. In the end I went back to bed. A week later my mother received a telegram telling us that Maurice had been killed on the Somme. I never told her about the voice in the night but I worked out that I had heard it the night he died.'

She was still holding the two pictures, the framed photograph of her brother and the painting of the boy with the flower. As she clutched them against her, the children saw a tear trickle slowly down one cheek.

Nobody spoke for a while, then Floss said timidly, 'Miss Adeline, do you really think the timing of that was significant? I mean, it might have been coincidence, mightn't it?'

'I don't think it was,' Magnus said firmly.

At first the old lady said nothing. 'Could you reach for my handkerchief?' she eventually asked Floss. 'It's in the pocket of my blouse. I can't seem to...' She was still clutching the two pictures. Floss found the hanky, a soft square of checked cotton, and gently dabbed at the papery cheeks.

'Thank you, dear. Let me go on. Yes, I think it probably was significant. The Lady Alice Neale seems to be mourning over some lost loved one. I think it is her son, and I think her son is this child, the little boy holding the flower. That night in

1916, when my brother lost his life, I believe that her mourning became ours, across the centuries. I suppose, in a way, she was trying to communicate with me. And now, nearly a hundred years later, she is still in mourning, still not at rest. So many people, if they have not actually seen her, like Magnus, have heard the same voice.

'*Canst thou not minister to a mind diseased*

Pluck from the memory a rooted sorrow...'

Her voice wavered, then ceased, and she stared sadly down at the knotted web her gnarled hands had made round the pictures.

'That's *Macbeth*,' Floss said in surprise.

'It is. Clever girl.'

'No, I'm not. Magnus seems to know the whole play off by heart. It's just that I'm trying to learn some of it, to get a part in a play at school. It's what the doctor says to Macbeth, when Lady Macbeth is sleep walking.'

'It is indeed. It's about guilt. It's about terrible deeds that prey on the mind and will not let you rest.'

Magnus was thinking hard about the face of the Lady Alice Neale. In the portrait it was hard and truculent, unforgiving, almost cruel, the face of a woman who might be capable of wicked things. And yet, the second time he had seen her, through the door at the swimming pool, he had seen other things in the face, traces of sorrow and regret under the stubborn exterior. He said, 'But what is Lady Alice supposed to have *done*, Miss Adeline? What is it that she weeps about, after nearly four hundred years? Why is she guilty?'

'Well, there are all kinds of theories, some of them rather wild, but there is a very strong tradition that she killed one of her own sons, or at least, neglected him in some way that led to his death. As you know, there is no record of such a son or of such a death, there is no tomb, but the story has persisted for nearly four centuries, as you've just pointed out, and when a story really persists like that you begin to think there might be some truth behind it.'

'You mean "No smoke without a fire"?' suggested Magnus.

'That's one way of putting it. The Neale family were very clever people and that's historical fact. You can look it up. They produced all kinds of scholars and one or two high-powered diplomats, and they were very close to the king. They think that a Neale – possibly a brother of Lady Alice – tutored young Edward the Sixth, the son of Henry the Eighth, who died young. There's no hard evidence but there *is* evidence that Elizabeth the First spent some time at the Abbey and was friends with Lady Alice Neale.'

At this point she stopped abruptly. Then she said, 'I think I can trust you, can't I?'

'Yes,' answered Magnus, stoutly. 'You certainly

can.' But Floss, wondering what on earth was coming next, did not answer. She was too excited.

'Florence, there's a tiny picture on the wall by that window... no... have you got it? It's a piece of tapestry work in a frame. Bring it to me, will you?'

The cloth square was black silk, richly worked in gold, vine leaves and grapes, exquisitely embroidered, the detail so fine it looked as if it had been executed by fairy-tale mice in a story book.

'This relic has always been in our family,' said Miss Adeline. 'And it is supposed to have come from a dress worn by Elizabeth the First, when she was at the Abbey. Now of course nobody can prove that, but if you go to the National Portrait Gallery in London you will see her wearing such a dress. What is one to make of it? I don't think I know.

'As I said, the Neales were clever people, the women as well as the men, but one son – if he existed at all – seems to have been a severe disappointment to his ambitious parents. He may have had what I believe you now call 'learning difficulties', perhaps he just couldn't spell.'

'I can't spell,' Floss said quite belligerently. 'It doesn't mean you're thick. It's just the way your brain works.'

'Oh, I know dear, and listen, good news. I can't spell, either. It must be in the family. You and I must be related, way back. He may have been, what's the word these days, dyslexic, or he could have been educationally sub-normal. Feeble-minded is how people used to put it. Whatever the truth of the matter, such a child would have been a very great embarrassment in a distinguished and clever family like the Neales, especially one that was connected with royalty.

'The tradition is that his father, determined to make something of him, drove him very, very hard, that he was confined in a school room for long hours, to work over his books. A tutor – possibly the royal one, who would have been his uncle – seems to have intervened and pleaded for him, even tried to get him away from here, at night, through a tunnel under the river.'

'A *what*?' Floss interrupted. This was getting more and more fantastic. 'Is the tunnel still there?' She noticed that Magnus had gone very silent, which was odd. She would have thought the existence of a tunnel might have sparked off more of his penetrating questions.

'Oh yes, I think so. I used to play in it, with Maurice. Hasn't Maude mentioned it? Well, I suppose she might not have done. I used to have a key... But let me get on with the story, I'm losing the thread. We don't know what happened to the tutor. The Neales were a determined and ambitious pair. They wouldn't have cared for a young whippersnapper interfering. They may well have got rid of him. Perhaps he gossiped, about their harsh methods with their son.'

'Who was in charge really?' asked Floss. 'Do we know?'

'Well, no. The husband was very much older than the wife, she was only fifteen when he married her, and from his portrait – we don't have it in the Abbey, it's in a gallery in Edinburgh for some reason – he looks even tougher than she does, if you can imagine that. So perhaps she was very much under his influence. She was very, very young to be a mother. She may even have been frightened of him. Perhaps he beat her, as well as his children.'

'Please tell us what happened to the little boy, Miss Adeline,' said Magnus. Floss looked sharply at him because his voice sounded lost and curiously detached. He was doing his staring into space act again, his looking at nothing.

'Well, the boy disappeared and it was obviously a scandal at the time. That's why, if he existed at all, all records of him have been expunged, apart from this one picture which many believe to be his likeness and has been catalogued as William Neale. He's always referred to as William, by the way.'

'What happened to him?' repeated Magnus in the same dull voice, almost as if he didn't really want to know the answer.

'Well, everyone has their own theory. One is that he was locked in his room with his books and that he simply got forgotten. Perhaps his mother went riding in the woods, met the young Queen Elizabeth, and ended up at Windsor for the night. It's not far from here. She was extremely grand after all, and she could have easily thought someone in the house was seeing to the child. Don't forget that it was a very large family and a very large house, and that there would have been dozens of servants. Such an aristocratic woman wouldn't have seen very much of her children. It just could have happened that way.

'Anyway, tradition has it – and that's all it is, tradition, we have no proof – that he was found dead, in a locked room, after three days, because nobody knew he was there. It really might have been an accident. They think terrified servants disposed of the body, but it's pure speculation. Nobody knows. Another theory, and the only other credible one, to me, is that she killed him herself, not deliberately of course, but through losing her temper. You only have to look at her to see that there's an awful lot of violence in her face, suppressed violence, the sort that's kept under control most of the time but can be really terrible if it ever breaks out. She could have become so infuriated with his stupidity that she boxed his ears rather too hard – you know, beat him about the head and caused a brain haemorrhage. Or perhaps they were both cruel to him, perhaps she did what she did under the husband's influence. It can happen you know… well it *has* happened. You only need open the newspaper to see what terrible things people do to children – not always by accident, either. I personally think—'

But Floss interrupted. 'Magnus?' she said. 'Magnus? Are you all right?' and she turned in panic to the old lady. 'Can you wait a minute, Miss Adeline, I don't think he's very well… *Magnus*!'

But Magnus didn't hear her, or anyone. His head had begun to swim round, then there was a fine tingling sensation in his joints and he suddenly felt horribly nauseous. But before he could be sick he had crashed forwards in a dead faint.

VIII

'**M**iss Adeline, he's fainted! What should I *do*?' Floss could hear that her own voice was shrill with panic. Nobody had ever fainted on her before and Magnus had hit the floor with an almighty thump. What a good thing the drawing room was carpeted, not tiled, like the hall. He could have injured himself terribly if he'd hit his head on something hard. He could have died, like the little boy who couldn't spell.

'It's all right,' said the old lady from her chair. 'Give me my bag. It's hanging on that chair. Thank you.' While she was opening it she gave Floss calm instructions. 'Sit on the floor with him. Now pull him up towards you and let him lean against your knees. Make a seat. Have you done that?'

'Nearly. Just let me… that's it. Got him,' Floss said, puffing and blowing. Magnus was very light but he felt like an absolute dead weight in her arms.

'Now, push his head down between his knees,

no, *right* down. You must bring the blood back to his head. And here, make him take a good sniff of these, they're smelling salts. They'll help. It's only a faint, Florence. It's probably a bit too stuffy for him in here. I feel the cold dreadfully, I'm afraid, so I keep it rather warm. Ah good. He's coming round already.'

Magnus, sniffing at the small green flask which Floss was holding under his nose, was making little moaning noises. Then he gave a sudden sneeze and looked round. 'Where... what happened?' he said. 'Why am I on the floor?'

'Just a little faint, Magnus. No harm done. No, don't get up yet, sit down there with Florence until you've got your sea-legs back again.' Miss Adeline sounded vigorous and young, not like the little old woman she actually was, all but invisible in her deep fireside chair, but the lively girl who had gone round to the bedsides of wounded soldiers, plumping up their pillows and bathing their foreheads.

'I suddenly felt sick,' he said. 'I think I need some fresh air.'

The electric kettle, long since forgotten in the adjoining kitchen, had filled the low room with steam, reminding Magnus of the tea which was to accompany the carefully arranged bread and butter. The very thought of it made his stomach heave and he brought his hand up to his mouth.

'I've got to get out of this room,' he whispered

to Floss. 'I'll throw up if I don't get outside.'

Miss Adeline, who had heard this, put the smelling salts back in her bag and slowly zipped it shut. 'Perhaps you had better go home my dears,' she said kindly. 'I suspect we've talked enough for one day. But take your time, Magnus, don't rush. Let your body adjust. A faint is always a little warning to us. Have you been overdoing things, I wonder?'

He stared at her blankly, on his feet again now but rocking slightly, trying in his mind to reach back to what they had been talking about before the darkness had come up and washed him away. Now he remembered. She had been telling them about the little boy who'd been confined in a dark space and perhaps even beaten to death by his own mother and father. The fainting was not exactly 'a warning' but he understood what she was saying, that he had reacted with his body to something which his mind felt was too painful to bear.

He was feeling distinctly odd and his mind was fuzzy. He tried hard to recall the exact details of what Miss Adeline had told him so that he could write them down the minute he got back to the turret room, but he found that his brain wasn't processing things properly. He simply couldn't assemble the facts in any order and now he was developing quite a nasty headache.

All he knew was that talking with Miss Adeline had filled in some vital missing pieces of the jigsaw of events that had centred on the ghostly walk of Lady Alice Neale, and that what she had told them must be thought about again, and talked over. But it was as if one part of him didn't want to do this, because it meant going back into his own past, the most horrific part of it where the pain and suffering was. Nobody else in the world knew that – unless it was Lady Alice herself.

Slowly the sick feeling left him and after he had sat quietly for ten minutes, they said goodbye to Miss Adeline and left her sitting in her green wing chair, eating bread and butter and sipping the tea which Floss had made, from one of her beautiful old cups. She had insisted that Floss took Magnus home, to lie down. But they had promised to come back in the morning if he felt better. She said she had more to tell them, if they cared to hear.

And Magnus had said yes, oh, yes please, anything she could remember. Before the fainting, he had particularly wanted to ask about the key to the tunnel, but he'd thought it better to wait until she volunteered more information herself. If she really trusted them she would tell them about it in due course. He very much wanted to find the tunnel, but it seemed too much to hope that it wouldn't have been blocked up years ago.

Floss said, as they walked towards the Abbey, 'I do think you should lie down, Mags. You've gone terribly pale. I'll come up with you. I can sit and read.' She thought she might have a look at the sleep-walking scene in the play. How astonishing that the old lady should have quoted that. 'A rooted sorrow' was what had caused Lady Macbeth to walk in her sleep, wringing her hands and trying to wash the blood away. The Lady Alice Neale seemed similarly tormented.

As they approached the Abbey buildings they saw that someone had unloaded a lot of building equipment at the base of the turret. There were neat stacks of heavy planks, and a concrete mixer and a huge pile of sand under the trees. There were serious-looking electrical machines, too, amongst them was a drill, the kind used for breaking up pavements.

Magnus, whose cheeks were still pale, looked at all the equipment very carefully as they walked past towards the front door. 'I should think they're going to dig into the base of the turret,' he said. 'They'd need a big drill for that.'

'Why, Mags? Isn't it unstable already, because of its foundations drying out after all the heat waves? Won't drilling make it worse?'

'That's exactly it. It *will* be unstable and one way of making sure it doesn't fall down is to dig round the base, make some holes, and fill them with concrete. I think it's called "underpinning". The Colonel's been given a grant to pay for it, according to Wilf. But he can't have known they were going to start so soon. Surely he wouldn't have allowed us to sleep up there if he'd known.'

'How do you know about under-pinning?' asked Floss. Magnus's amazing general knowledge continued to surprise her. But she wasn't going to say so. She didn't want him to clam up on her.

He said quite casually, 'Father Godless, that old priest I used to know, had a church that was falling down, and that was very ancient too. They underpinned it, to give it new foundations. There had to be some excavating first.'

'I see. So do you think they'll put us in one of those portakabins?'

'I don't know. Wilf says they're very damp and that there's mould on the walls. I suppose we could always go in the flat, with the Colonel and Cousin M.'

'I don't think there's any room,' Floss said. 'It's pretty small. If we want to watch TV, Cousin M said that the best place is in Wilf's kitchen. It's a bit odd, making us watch in a kitchen when she's got a television in her sitting room, don't you think? She's so friendly to us in every other way.'

Magnus said, as they toiled up the spiral staircase to the dormitory, 'Don't you think it's because of Colonel Stickley? He really doesn't want us around, does he? He's trying to make sure that we stay out of the way.' But he was thinking hard about the Colonel's missing son. He'd decided that the old man couldn't bear to be reminded of him, not knowing whether he was alive or dead, and that this was the main reason he was being so off-hand with the three of them.

'Do you really want to move out of this room, Mags?' Floss said, wandering round it and looking appreciatively at the pretty curtains and bedcovers, the view of the river through the deep windows, the curious curved walls. 'Does it make you feel funny, when you think about that girl falling out of the window?'

Magnus considered this, as he closed his eyes and got comfortable on his bed. 'No. I've changed my mind, actually. I'd rather stay now. Wouldn't you?'

Floss hesitated. Then she said, 'Yes, I think I would. Though I was a bit scared when I heard the voice. But it's funny, I've got used to the idea of Lady Alice being around, now. I feel almost as if we ought *not* to move rooms.'

'I feel that,' Magnus replied. 'It's as if there was a purpose behind it, us coming here, to the Abbey. I do think something might happen, even if it takes ages.' And he thought again about ghost-spotting being like bird-watching, and about sitting tight and waiting.

Waves of tiredness seemed to be lapping gently over him and he knew he was falling asleep. 'You don't have to stay here,' he said to Floss. 'Go and find Sam. I'll come down when I wake up.'

'I'm staying,' Floss said firmly. 'I don't want you fainting again, up here on your own, without me.'

Magnus was pleased because this meant that Floss cared about him. He started to say, 'Thanks, Floss,' but he fell asleep before he got the words out.

She crept past him and squatted in front of the big fireplace. The piece of sticking plaster he had fixed across the crack looked just the same. But now she had time to examine it, she could see that it was all rather alarming. Certainly she'd be worried if such a big crack appeared in one of their bedroom walls at home, worried in case a heavy lorry went past and sent the wall collapsing into the road below.

She rummaged in her suitcase until she found a wire coathanger. These were very useful objects in their house. Mum used them to unblock the sink, and once she'd seen her father get into his locked car with one. Burglars must find them very handy. Carefully, she untwisted the hanger until she had a straight sharp piece of wire. Then she stuck the end of it through the crack, just above Magnus's strip of sticking plaster. She was amazed at how far it went in, before meeting solid wall. Before she withdrew it she wiggled it about to try and get a feel for how much space there was, inside the crack, and there was obviously quite a lot. The walls of the turret, the very oldest part of the Abbey, were terrifically thick.

When she tried to pull the coat hanger out again, she discovered it was stuck. She must have bent it somehow. She tugged and tugged and bits of plaster fell off the wall, but she couldn't get it to come out. So she pushed it further in, to free it, and the whole thing suddenly disappeared into the crack. She actually heard it fall down into the darkness with a tinny clatter.

A wave of real fear hit her then, fear that clutched at her throat, and all because of a crack in an old wall. Something she'd once read in a fairy story came into her head, nagged at her, and wouldn't leave her alone. 'The inside is bigger than the outside.' But what did it mean exactly?

She settled down on the floor next to the sleeping Magnus and opened a book, not *Macbeth*, that was too scary, but a favourite, reassuring school story she had read many times before. She wasn't going to admit it to anybody but she was frightened lest the crack in the fireplace might widen to admit into the room the Lady Alice Neale.

IX

'Floss! Mags!,

Floss opened her eyes, feeling very stiff. She was still sitting on the floor with her back against Magnus's bed, her school story open at page one. She must have dozed off before the end of the first paragraph. No wonder, it was incredibly hot, even in this thick-walled turret room.

'That's Sam,' said Magnus, getting off his bed and crossing over to the window. 'He's sitting by the river.'

'Grub up!' he was shouting, then, 'Light repast! Come and get it!' Magnus could see him waving a jug.

They made their way down the spiral staircase along the cool passages and past Balaam's donkey, forever bowing low before the angel, past Pontius Pilate, then out across the baked lawns. Arthur emerged from under some bushes and streaked in front of them, his pale gingery fur hardly distinguishable against the browning grass. 'You can really see where the first Abbey buildings were now,' Magnus observed. 'Look, those lines show where the walls must have been. Cousin Maude said it sometimes happens, when the ground gets very dry.'

'It's stifling,' Floss said. 'Do you think it's to do with the ozone layer?'

'I don't know. But the lack of rain's got to be the explanation for all those cracks in the turret. Did you see the builder's stuff, Sam?'

'Yes. Suppose that means they'll put us somewhere else.'

'Not necessarily. They'll only be digging outside. And nothing's going to fall down in a hurry.'

'I'm glad about that.' Sam was trying to prise the lid off a tin. 'Want a flapjack?' The top of the tin was embellished with labrador puppies. 'Honestly, these puppies are wearing *bows*. I bet it's Maude's tin. I bet she'd give Arthur a bow.' He offered Magnus the flapjack.

'I don't think I'll have any,' he said. 'I still feel a bit queasy. I'll just have some of the lemonade.'

'He fainted at Miss Adeline's,' Floss explained.

'Really? What was it like?' Sam was envious. He'd never fainted himself. It seemed to him that it was always the sensitive, delicate people who passed out, not the cloddish ones like him.

'Not great,' Magnus said shortly. 'How did you get on in the village?'

Sam leaned back against a massive cedar tree

that was spreading long shadows over the scorched grass. 'Not bad. I discovered quite a lot actually. You ought to come and see the Neale memorial in the church, it's really hideous, like something out of *Madame Tussaud's*. The whole family's in it, all kneeling under a great big canopy and all looking terribly holy, and there are loads of dogs and things, and loads of children.'

'How many?' asked Magnus.

'Don't remember, but loads, all lolling around. It's quite funny. There's a baby all squashed up by Lady Neale's feet. I thought it was a dog at first. The canopy makes it look as if they're all in bed.'

'I suppose the idea is that they're waiting to be transported to heaven,' said Magnus. 'Was one of the children called William by any chance?'

'I don't know. All the inscriptions were in Latin.'

Floss interrupted. 'William's not included in the memorial, Mags. Miss Adeline told us that.'

'I know. But I thought they might have put a baby in as a kind of symbol, you know, *code*.'

'Who's William?' asked Sam, not understanding any of this.

'He was one of Lady Alice's sons, and they think she might have killed him, or that his parents killed him between them.'

'Why? What on earth for?'

'Because he was thick, because he couldn't

131

spell, or blotted his books, that kind of thing,' said Floss casually.

'*Really*? He was bumped off because he was thick?'

'Yes, really. Though there's a lot more to it than that, according to Miss Adeline.' Floss was enjoying imparting this information to the astonished Sam. But Magnus stood up suddenly, scooped up Arthur and walked with him down to the river.

Sam's eyes followed him along the grass. 'What's up with him? Has he taken the huff again?'

Floss could feel herself going red. 'I don't know. Perhaps I've been tactless, just coming out with it like that. He was OK with Miss Adeline, in fact we were getting on really well with her. That is, until she told us the story of this dead boy, and the theories about him. Then, well he just passed out. I suppose it reminded him of when he was little, and the way he was treated. But she wasn't to know, she was sweet,' she added loyally.

'So are you saying that this Lady Alice person walks about wailing and moaning because she accidentally killed her son, for being stupid?'

'Well, it's one of the theories, apparently. I thought you didn't believe in ghosts?'

'I don't.' But then Sam decided he'd better come clean and tell her what he'd discovered. 'The people round here obviously do, though, like mad. I found a guidebook in the church. It doesn't say much, it's mainly about the area, about the local walks and things, but it *does* say that the Abbey's "the most haunted building in England".'

'If you believe in hauntings,' said Floss. 'I wish you could see Lady Alice for yourself. You're like Doubting Thomas in the Bible.'

Magnus, still cuddling Arthur, was walking slowly back towards them.

'He says ghost-hunting's like bird-watching,' she whispered.

'What have birds got to do with it?'

'Just that you have to be patient.'

'There's a tunnel under the river,' Floss said very casually, staring down towards the water, 'Miss Adeline told us about it'.

'There can't be,' said Sam.

'Why not? There's the Mersey Tunnel and there's the Blackwall Tunnel. They go under rivers and they're huge. And look at the Channel Tunnel. That goes under an entire *sea*,' she pointed out.

'Yes. But here? What on earth for?'

'Well, think about it,' said Magnus quietly. 'Think of the days when people were being persecuted for their religion. They used to hide priests in holes and things. People were shut in them for weeks sometimes. So why not an actual tunnel? You had a chance of escaping to freedom then.'

'It just sounds a bit far-fetched to me, that's all,'

Sam said, but less confidently now.

So Floss explained. 'One of the theories about the little boy who died is that his tutor might have tried to get him away from the Abbey altogether, down the tunnel. That's what Miss Adeline told us. She definitely believes in it, well, she actually said she used to play in it with her brother. So it's got to be true. She's absolutely in her right mind, Sam.'

'I'd quite like to come with you, next time you go,' Sam muttered. He felt embarrassed now. If there really *was* a tunnel he'd certainly like to explore it, and if she'd told them so much about the Abbey then this particular old lady must still have all her faculties, not like his Aunt Helen.

'We're going back in the morning,' said Magnus. 'We promised.'

They watched television that night, in the flat shared by Cousin Maude and Colonel Stickley. He had obviously relented – or Cousin Maude had drawn the line at the three children watching Wilf's tiny black-and-white set, in the kitchen. Nothing was said about the builders. They had brought all their equipment and then gone away again. The three children had agreed not to raise the matter themselves. After all, they might have gone home before the men came back again.

Nobody was concentrating very hard on what

was on television. It was too hot and they all kept dozing off, Cousin Maude over a piece of embroidery and the Colonel over his chess game with Sam. He'd been terrified when the old man had offered him a game, but he'd found his elderly opponent very patient, even a little encouraging. Floss cuddled Arthur who watched the television intently, with appreciative bursts of purring.

Magnus's mind was busy somewhere else, systematically going through all they'd learned so far about the Abbey and all that had happened since they'd arrived. Pretending to watch an inane TV programme on a flickering screen was a good chance to escape into one's private thoughts.

He went to bed early and immediately fell into a very deep sleep. Sam and Floss were more wakeful, Sam because he was hot and Floss because she was nervous of that long dark crack in the fireplace, down which the coat hanger had disappeared. Part of her felt brave, though, and wanted to see the Lady Alice Neale face-to-face, as Magnus claimed to have done.

But ghost-spotting was like bird-watching according to him and that night, although she watched very carefully, the birds never came.

X

After an undisturbed night's sleep, Magnus woke very early. When he opened his eyes the clock by his bed said it was only five-twenty. The others were still fast asleep, tucked up under their duvets. During the night the temperature had dropped sharply and delicious cool air was coming in through the open windows. Outside the birds were starting to tune up. The TV weatherman had said that today was going to be 'another scorcher'. Magnus got up at once, trying not to make any noise. This might be the best part of the day and he was going to make the most of it.

Silently, he wriggled into his new swimming trunks – bright red with thin jazzy blue lines. He liked them a lot, the children's mother had bought them for him when she bought the dressing gown. She always picked things he liked; she was a brilliant person.

He rolled up a towel, tucking his shorts inside it, pulled on a T-shirt and sandals and crept towards the door. Then he remembered his tell-tale piece of sticking plaster, went back to the fireplace and inspected it. In the dim early light, he couldn't really be sure, but it did seem to him to have become very slightly stretched, if only by a couple of millimetres. He must note this down, in the exercise book.

Unknown to the others he'd already written an account of the three apparitions he'd seen: the empty frame, the woman with no feet, and the shimmering white shape that had floated across the swimming pool. To the list he'd added the wreckage in the fireplace and the scattered white petals. They must surely be to do with her too. Miss Adeline's brother had been killed in the month of July, and on the night of his death she had heard Lady Alice's voice. The rare, old-fashioned flowers, which resembled the modern peony, she obviously associated with her son, and the flowers bloomed in July. And the three of them, three modern children, one of whom had suffered like William Neale, were now in this house, in July. Magnus believed it was their presence which had made her active again and more especially, *his* presence.

Would she be in the swimming pool building again? That was surely too much to hope. But the more he thought about it the more convinced he was that she was trying to communicate with him, that she'd been seeking his help.

Running down the turret spiral staircase, he walked out into the early summer sunshine, across the dewy grass and along the gravelled drive. Then, very cautiously, he approached the swimming pool building where all seemed deserted, except that somebody had come and propped the outer door open, presumably to freshen the air. The dried-up potted plants inside made the muggy atmosphere feel stale and there was a faint smell of putrefaction overlaid with the smell of chlorine.

Through the glass of the inner door he saw someone walking towards the deep end. Magnus would have liked to be able to dive in, but he'd only recently learned to swim, and he lacked confidence. This man was obviously planning to take a dive though. He couldn't see his face yet but the lean skinny body was definitely that of Colonel Stickley. His pronounced limp was unmistakeable. At the end of the pool the old man bent down and began to unwind a broad flesh-coloured bandage that had been wrapped round his right leg, just above the knee. Carefully he folded up the bandage and put it on a bench then, holding on to a metal railing, he removed the lower part of his leg and propped it against the wall. Then he dived into the pool with a great splash and began to swim, awkwardly, with a lot of rolling from side-to-side, but quite fast.

'That's brilliant,' Magnus said, and he must

have spoken it out loud, because behind him Wilf said , 'Not bad, is it? He can swim A lot faster than me. He lost the leg in forty-three. Couldn't swim before then, fear of water, that kind of thing. Just shows, doesn't it?'

'Yes it does,' muttered Magnus, watching Colonel Stickley do a neat turn and set off again down the pool. Something was making him want to cry, the plastic leg propped carefully against the wall, that brave, ungainly dive.

Wilf said, 'Listen, go and have a swim yourself. Just keep over to the other side, there's plenty of room, he won't even notice. Anyway, there'll be others here soon. This is the day your cousin Maude offered it to the village folk. One or two usually show up.'

'Are you sure?' Magnus said, rather doubtfully. He didn't want Colonel Stickley to shout at him, but the water did look very inviting.

'Yes. It'll be OK. And if he blows his top I'll deal with him. But he'll be out in a few minutes. He never notices anything when he's swimming, anyhow. He has to concentrate.'

Magnus waited until the Colonel had done another two lengths, had made his turn and had his back to him. Then he slipped into the water at the shallow end and set off cautiously. He'd only once managed a whole length, and he was still very nervous. He kept putting one foot on the bottom, for reassurance, and when he was half-way down, and the floor disappeared, he held on to the curved tiles that jutted out just above the water. This way, first hopping and then clinging, he made his way to the deep end. Then, equally cautious, he turned and began to go back. It was not exactly swimming, but he felt it was giving him confidence. He loved the feel of the water on his body and the fact that he virtually had the pool to himself.

But soon it began to fill up. He saw the Colonel get out, bandage his false leg in position and limp away towards the changing rooms. But the old man was replaced by others, equally old, even ancient, some of them. And they all seemed to be women.

Magnus stuck to his lane by the wall and watched them going sedately up and down. Two, who swam together, had carefully piled-up grey hair and they progressed very slowly, with fixed, flat smiles, as if the main business of their lives was to avoid getting their perfect hair wet. Another was small and stringy with a great hooked nose. She wore a most elaborate bathing cap, purple with a swag of yellow swathed round it, rising to a point, a hat that might have been worn at the court of some Eastern potentate, and she swam up and down grim-faced, counting her strokes aloud. Once, somebody swimming very slowly got in her way and she barked, 'Stick to your own lane, *please*!' She was terrifying. And she got even madder when the two ladies with hair-dos stopped to gossip in the shallow end, leaning lazily back and letting their substantial legs float out in front of them, inevitably blocking her progress. They looked so relaxed as they chatted away that Magnus half expected them to produce flasks of coffee, or to light cigarettes.

When he got out of the pool, they waved to him and one shouted, 'Nice to have some young round here, for a change. What's your name, darling?' but Magnus, suddenly shy, scuttled off to get changed.

As he rubbed himself dry he found that it was hard, now, to believe in his first visit to this pool when, across the shimmering water, he had perceived the shape of the Lady Alice Neale, and heard her voice. It felt already as if it belonged to another time, almost as if it had never happened. Perhaps it had not. Feeling unpleasantly damp, he walked back slowly to the tower, fighting with an inexplicable feeling of loss, and of disappointment.

Floss and Sam were awake now and rather irritable. The builders had obviously come back and the noise of them unloading more equipment at the foot of the turret, had broken into their sleep. As Magnus entered the room, there was a great thumping sound from down below and it seemed as if the whole building shook.

'I think they'll *have* to move us out, if it's going

to be like that all the time,' Sam said. 'Thought this was a restoration. They seem to be hell-bent on knocking it all down, to me.'

'I've told you,' Magnus reminded him. 'They fill holes up with concrete so they have to make the holes first.'

'In other words, it gets worse before it gets better?'

'Something like that.'

'Great.'

Sam was grumpy not only because the builders had woken him up but also because Magnus had beaten him to the swimming pool. Not that it sounded a very attractive proposition, swimming up and down with a lot of old-age pensioners trying not to get their hair wet.

'The Colonel's got an artificial leg,' Magnus was telling Floss. 'He sort of, unwrapped it, before he dived in.'

'Ugh!'

But Magnus said loyally, 'I think it's rather brave of him. I mean, nobody can help having a look at a thing like that. It must be awful for him.'

At breakfast, Colonel Stickley made no reference to seeing Magnus in the pool, just as he'd never referred to their meeting in the night, in the Great Hall, under the empty frame, nor was there any reference to the arrival of the builders. He seemed particularly bad-tempered, snapping at Maude for leaving a spoon stuck in the marmalade jar, and sweeping Arthur off the table, knocking him away sharply with the back of his hand, just as he'd managed to reach the butter dish.

"I'm sorry, dears,' Maude said in embarrassment, as the lean, upright figure stomped off, muttering bad-temperedly under his breath. 'He's terribly upset. He received a letter in yesterday's post about his son. Well, *not* about his son, that's the point. He'd been waiting for news. There've been government representations in London and he'd worked so hard to get them to do something, and now – nothing. He's going up to London this morning, to talk to somebody in one of the foreign embassies.'

'Miss Adeline said she thought his son must be dead,' Floss told her. 'What do you think, Maude?'

'I really don't know, dear. It does seem very unlikely that he would be alive after all this time. But we have to go on hoping. After all, no actual death has been reported and no body has been found. Until it is, then there's still hope, I think.'

Magnus suddenly thought about the son of Lady Alice Neale. 'Cousin Maude,' he said, 'did they ever find the body of that boy who died here, the one Miss Adeline told us about?'

She shrugged. 'Not that I know of. There's nothing about him in the parish records, or in the family memorial. But of course we don't actually know that he ever existed. It's just rumour – well, tradition's a better word.'

'But if he *did* exist and was killed, or died accidentally, they'd have had to bury him somewhere, wouldn't they?'

'Well, yes, except that if he'd died in some scandalous way I suppose they'd have disposed of his body pretty quickly. They'd have surely wanted to hush it up. They were very famous people in their day.

'And that's why the mother weeps,' Magnus said to himself. One thing at least had just slotted neatly into place. He'd talked a lot to Father Godless about ghosts, because of the troubles the old priest had had at his church. There were 'unquiet' ghosts, who walked the earth unhappily because nobody had ever laid them to rest, or because someone they loved had not been laid to rest. He saw it clearly now. The Lady Neale felt guilty about her son's death, and so she wept. But she also mourned because she had never said a proper goodbye to him. Perhaps terrified servants, finding him dead, had disposed of his body, then made up some story about how he had inexplicably disappeared. You *would* try and make up some kind of story, faced with a formidable woman like Lady Alice Neale.

'I thought that this afternoon we might take a boat along the river and have a picnic,' Cousin Maude said. 'There's a dinghy here and Wilf keeps it in good order. He could come with us, while the Colonel's in London. There's a swimming place too, and it's a bit more fun than the pool. Do you fancy that at all?'

'Great!' said Sam and Floss together.

'Yes. Thank you,' Magnus said, but more slowly. It was the tunnel under the river that really interested him, not taking a boat out. Still, it was just possible that she might have some information about the tunnel herself – or Wilf might.

After breakfast and the ritual washing of hands (which oddly, they all dutifully performed, even in Colonel Stickley's absence) they set off to see Miss Adeline. This time her front door was propped open by a cast-iron figure of Mr Punch, painted bright fairground colours.

'We still ought to knock,' Floss said. 'It's rude, just barging in.' So they let the polished brass knocker rise and fall three times. As before, there was silence, but finally they heard her voice. 'Is that the children? Is it Magnus and Florence, and is Samuel with you today?'

'Yes, I'm here,' said Sam, feeling a bit as though he was reporting for duty. But the old woman's voice sounded so firm and youthful that he was a bit ashamed that he'd not come last time.

'Well, come and join me in the drawing room. There are cold drinks. It's too hot for coffee.'

As they walked down the tiled passageway, Arthur, who had followed them from the Abbey, suddenly bounded ahead, looking like a tiny fox, with the fat bush of his tail beating the air impatiently as he sought out Miss Adeline. When they reached the drawing room he was already settled in her lap and purring loudly.

'Maude tells me that this is a beautiful cat,' the old lady said, pulling gently at his ears, 'but my goodness, he's got a round little tummy.'

'He's a big eater,' Floss explained. 'He's always ravenous.'

'My eyes are pretty useless these days, but I can see that he's a very special colour. There are so many varieties of orange cat, aren't there – and they're always male by the way – as many varieties of colour as there are kinds of marmalade. Do you like marmalade, Samuel?' she said. 'I'm sorry you missed tea yesterday. Magnus also missed tea, as it happens, but he was unwell, so it was hardly his fault.'

Samuel, like Magnus the day before, wondered whether the old lady was playing some kind of game with him. He said, 'I don't like marmalade very much, it's too sour. I prefer peanut butter.'

This reply seemed quite satisfactory. 'Have a cold drink, all of you,' she said. 'I believe it's all set out in my kitchen. Maude came by with some things. She's so good. And there are biscuits. I would like one, if I may. I have a sweet tooth. No lemonade, though, it's a little too sour for me.' And she looked sideways at Sam, with a sly little smile, as if to say 'Your move.'

He decided to go for a safe, neutral remark, encouraged by Arthur, who was now trying to drape himself round the old lady's neck like a scarf. 'He really likes you,' he said, 'and he doesn't seem to like everybody.'

She smiled again. 'Well, cats are canny creatures. They respond to the good things in people but they sniff out the bad too.'

'He was terrified the night we came,' Magnus said. 'When I heard the woman crying and when the cold mist came, he sort of went rigid, then he bolted.'

'But were *you* afraid?' asked Miss Adeline.

'Only at first. Now I think she knows we're here. I think she may be trying to get through to us.'

'Yes. That may well be why you've come to the Abbey,' said Miss Adeline softly. 'I have noticed that she is always *most* active when there are young people around. That girl who fell from the window could have been indulging in wild horseplay – and thank God she wasn't killed – but it could have been something to do with Lady Alice. She might have simply terrified the girl out of her wits.'

She turned to Sam. 'I notice that, so far, you have said nothing Samuel. I'm just wondering why you are sitting there so quietly. Do you think all this is sheer gobbledegook?'

'Not necessarily,' Sam said, cautiously. 'It's just that I've never seen a ghost.'

'But neither have I.'

'*I* don't expect to.'

'Fair enough. So, do you find all this talk rather tiresome?'

'Oh no. As a matter of fact I think the whole theory of ghosts is quite interesting, in itself. But you don't have to believe it's true. It's like religion, in that way.'

'Do you know anything of the theory, Samuel?'

'Well, I do know it's all to do with time, so that when, for example, a ghost walks through a wall, it's because, in their time, the wall wasn't there. But it's more complicated than that, isn't it? I heard someone say once that we are ghosts ourselves and that our lives have already happened, that somebody's just playing them back to us, perhaps the very people we think of as "ghosts". I get lost at that point.'

'I think we all do, Samuel,' said Miss Adeline. 'So, what else can you tell me about ghosts?'

'Well, I've noticed that ghost stories are nearly always about horrible things, brutal murders and ghastly accidents. There don't seem to be many nice ghosts around, quietly minding their own business. Ghosts are always banging and thumping and rattling their chains – or crying, like the ghost in the Abbey.'

Magnus said, 'That's because violence always

seems to attract them. I mean, when something awful has happened in a place it's as if the stones themselves absorb it. It doesn't seem to settle down into history in the same way as an ordinary, peaceful event. Sometimes, like in the Abbey, it *never* seems to settle down.'

'Unless—' began Miss Adeline.

'Unless what?' Magnus demanded. He really sounded quite rude. But she'd made exactly this kind of tantalizing remark yesterday.

'Unless the dead are laid to rest.'

'But we don't even know if there is a 'dead'. I mean, that boy William Neale may never have existed. It could all be made up.' Magnus was feeling more and more frustrated now. He felt like screaming.

The old lady withdrew into her deep wing chair and sat silent. The three children were silent too, and the atmosphere had definitely changed. There was a tension in the air, and a growing sense of expectancy.

After a few seconds, Miss Adeline sat forward and thrust her face up at them. 'Can I trust you?' she said, and Floss remembered that she had asked exactly the same question yesterday, before showing them the fragment of Queen Elizabeth's dress. But this time it sounded more like 'I have decided to trust you'. And she was right because, before they could reply, the old lady unzipped her bag which was sharing her lap with Arthur, and took out something wrapped in white tissue paper.

'This is the key to the tunnel under the river,' she said, 'and I believe' – and here she laughed to herself– 'that it may also be the key to the lifelong sorrows of the Abbey. But please, do be prepared to be disappointed. It's a very long time since anybody went there. I have held this key since my brother Maurice's death. Samuel, you are to have charge of it as you are the oldest of the three.'

Sam took the small white-wrapped parcel in trembling hands. 'But Miss Adeline, what are we actually looking for?'

'I am no longer sure. My brother put his childish treasures there once, in a chamber in the middle, where the river is deepest. There may still be something there… there may be other things, things I didn't know about… But I can't remember. Did I return alone, after his death? It's so very long ago… but there *was* something in the tunnel, some clue to it all.

'All I will tell you is that when you have found the answer, you will know that you have found it. And Samuel, I'm going to pray that you will. As you said, religion is interesting in itself but you don't have to believe that a word of it is true. It's just that I happen to believe that it is.'

XI

If Sam had been rather less excited at that moment he would have interpreted the old lady's last remark as a snub. But the weight of what felt like a very large key in his pocket was focusing his thoughts on other, more exciting things.

Firstly, there must *be* a tunnel, because here was the key to the entrance, a tunnel which went under a river, a proper tunnel made with hands, not something bored out by machines to get cars in a quick orderly fashion from A to B. Secondly, this tunnel was hundreds of years old and must have been there at least in the days of Elizabeth the First, if there was any truth in the story of the young tutor trying to get little William away from the Abbey.

Sam didn't really expect to find anything in the tunnel which would make particular sense of the ghost story, and of the figure of Lady Alice Neale which was supposed to haunt the Abbey, because he didn't believe in such things. He could see that

151

his sister might, and Magnus almost certainly did. Floss was romantic and saw things when she wanted to see them, and Magnus was beyond his understanding. Nothing about him was a surprise. What excited Sam about exploring the tunnel was very straightforward. It was, simply, that it was *there* like Mount Everest. It had the same fascination and challenge as a high mountain, or a seaside cave cut off at high tide, or a really massive tree which, merely to climb, was a complex and daring exercise.

He suspected that Magnus was probably furious at his being put in charge of the key because it was Magnus who had chatted up Miss Adeline. Floss was probably annoyed too, she'd think they should all be equally responsible for the key. In fact, she'd probably suggest they take turns to guard the key at nights. But as they walked back to the Abbey, Sam had a wicked but rather appealing thought. Why didn't he just slip off at some point and find the entrance to the tunnel on his own? They couldn't stop him He needn't even tell them where he was going.

It would have been horribly frustrating having to go sedately down the river with Wilf and Cousin Maude, had the tunnel entrance not been quite near the bank. This meant that the picnic expedition was a good chance to do a 'preliminary reconnoitre' as the Colonel might have put it.

Miss Adeline had told them that the tunnel

entrance had originally been in the house and that you got into it in one of the outlying cellars. But, long before her time, this internal entrance had been filled in. So that portion of the tunnel that went from the house to the river was inaccessible now, and nobody had ever excavated to find it. Her entrance, therefore, hers and Maurice's was a much later construction. She had told them to look for something flat, a lid with a ring set into it, and a lock. They might not need the key, she said. The lock might have corroded into nothing long ago.

After lunch, Wilf and Cousin Maude disappeared, Floss suspected for naps. She and Magnus snoozed for a bit, too, it was so hot and sticky they didn't have the energy to do much else. But Sam, desperate to be off, had paced about like something in a cage, checking every other minute on the key in his pocket. He went down to inspect progress at the foot of the turret, to pass the time, but discovered that the workmen, having constructed a temporary WC for themselves, and hidden it coyly under a tree, had gone away again.

An hour after lunch everybody met up outside the front door. Maude had brought rugs to sit on, and umbrellas. 'These are for the sun, dears,' she explained. 'I don't possess parasols, I'm not really the type.'

Floss felt Arthur suddenly brushing against her legs, then running in circles round them all, like a sheep dog herding them all together. 'He wants to come with us,' she said. 'Perhaps he thinks the picnic hamper's his basket.'

'It is, actually,' Cousin Maude said, slightly embarrassed. 'I gave it a good spring clean, though, before putting the sandwiches in.'

A five minute walk, under great trees, brought them to the river and to the boat. Even Magnus, who knew nothing about sailing, could see that the blue dinghy, which was called *Salut d'Amour*, was rather ancient. It had a wide-hipped, middle-aged appearance and was pleasantly battered-looking.

'She's watertight, if that's what you're wondering,' Wilf said, slightly on the defensive. He was fond of his old boat. 'Give me a hand with the basket, will you? Get in – you, too, Sam – and I'll hand it to you. Then we'll assist the ladies.'

'I can manage, thanks,' Floss said, hitching up her long cotton skirt and stepping straight in, rather heavily. The skirt, her last reminder of the bid to play Lady Macbeth, was pleasantly loose and cool. The boat rocked about and she sat down abruptly, feeling rather foolish. No sooner had she settled herself than Arthur took off from the bank and, with a flying leap, landed in a puddle at the bottom of the boat. They all laughed as he shook his small paws fastidiously.

'Arthur!' said Cousin Maude in dismay. 'You *can't* sail down the river with us. You can't swim and you hate water.'

'Oh, he can swim all right,' Wilf said, inspecting

the oars before fitting them into the rowlocks. 'Only cats don't *choose* to, that's the thing about cats. Let him come, he can only drown,' he added wickedly.

So they set off down the river, with Arthur draped across Floss's and Magnus's knees, making himself as long as possible because of the heat. Behind them sat Sam and opposite was Cousin Maude with the picnic hamper.

'I'll row to begin with, shall I?' suggested Wilf. 'Then someone else can take over. I don't mind. I quite fancy a lazy afternoon.'

'"While the Colonel's away, Wilf will play..."' said Floss cheekily.

'Something like that,' Wilf answered. 'He's staying up in London at his club for a few days. He's given me some time off.'

Magnus, who was getting very fond of Arthur, said, 'What if he does jump into the water? I couldn't fish him out, I can't swim that well, yet.'

'I'll save him,' Floss said. 'But he's already asleep. It didn't take him long, did it? He's pathetic.'

'No, he's just young, dear,' said Cousin Maude. 'He needs lots of little naps. So do the old folk,' and she laughed, then yawned.

It was peaceful, going slowly down the river, and cool for the first time since they'd come to the Abbey. They passed bright fields of wheat, already full and thick, then greener meadows where cows lay motionless, as if the heat made grazing itself too much of an effort. Gradually, the trees started to close in and Sam, who'd been delighted when Wilf had headed the boat away from the village and therefore in the direction prescribed by Miss Adeline, began to look carefully at the left-hand bank, the bank which formed the modern-day boundary of the Abbey grounds. He was to look for a stand of elm trees which was the first marker. Beyond these, Miss Adeline had explained, the vegetation became very dense and scrubby, 'a kind of wild shrubbery' was how she had described it. In the middle of this, fairly near the water's edge, they were to look out for some holly trees and that was where they would find the 'plate', which was the Victorian entrance to the tunnel.

Holly trees. Sam's heart had sunk when he'd heard that. He'd be scratched to bits trying to find what he was looking for. Were holly trees slow to grow? He very much hoped so. On the other hand they were fully grown trees when Miss Adeline was a girl, so with luck they might have died by now.

Taking a risk he said to Cousin Maude, 'Miss Adeline said there were some marvellous elm trees along this bit. Have we passed them yet?'

Maude, who had been dozing, perked up. 'Oh yes. I didn't know you were interested in trees, dear?'

'I am,' mumbled Sam, lying through his teeth and hoping the others wouldn't look at him.

'Well, I'm afraid they've gone, dear. Dutch elm disease. It was a terrible tragedy for the English countryside. Look, there are the stumps. You can see how massive the trees must have been. I fully intend to replace them, *and* to clear that tangle of bushes.'

Sam stared in dismay at the dense, dark mass of greenery that took up the river bank for several yards and stretched back from the water as far as the eye could see. He saw Magnus and Floss looking at it too, and he knew what they were all thinking, that hacking a way into that lot would be virtually impossible. They would need serious tools. Well, Wilf would have those, perhaps Cousin Maude had things too. But it was going to take them time, he could see that.

Wilf rowed on and they saw that, beyond the jungle of thick scrub, there was a fork in the river. The main waterway swept on, widening out and passing once more into dappled sunshine. But Wilf took the smaller tributary to the left, steering them under huge grey-green willows out of whose shade a family of ducks appeared, paddling gently on their way, just in front of the dinghy.

Floss clutched at Arthur, but he had seen them and had already taken up a tense crouching position on her lap. After watching them for a minute he stood up on her knees and made as if to dive in after them, but he stopped mid-way, his muscles suddenly frozen solid, making a defeated little growling noise.

'See what I mean?' Wilf said. 'He *knows* it's water and that it's bad news. He won't jump.'

'No, but he's going to be an awful nuisance,' Cousin Maude said. 'I think I'll have to pop home with him. He can go in his basket.'

'I'll take him,' Sam said, thinking that he could grab a sandwich, run home with Arthur, then come back to have a private look at that shrubbery.

Wilf was resting on his oars, letting the dinghy drift across what had turned into a pool though it was really a side shoot of the main river which had broadened out to make quite a respectable swimming place, at its broadest part almost the length of the Abbey pool. It ended in a wall of yellowish rock over which water trickled lazily.

'Don't be deceived,' Cousin Maude said. 'It can pour down over those rocks like Niagara, when we've had some rain.'

Wilf tied the dinghy to a tree trunk, drove a looped metal stake into the bank and secured it to that too. Then they all climbed out, Magnus and Sam handing up the basket and blankets, Floss proceeding very cautiously because Arthur was now struggling to get free.

'He'll get lost if we let him go,' Cousin Maude said. 'I should have shut him in the kitchen. He's not really old enough yet, to be independent.

That's how he got lost the day you arrived.'

'If you'll empty the basket I'll take him back now,' Sam offered.

'Will you bring my swimming things?' Floss said. 'I think I might go in later.'

'OK. What about you, Mags?'

'Don't think so.' Magnus didn't know how deep the pool was, and he didn't want to make a fool of himself in front of the others. He was planning to get a lot of practice in first.

Sam shut the lid of the basket down on the mewing kitten, equipped himself with a couple of sandwiches, slipped an apple in his pocket and set off in the direction of the Abbey.

He was able to walk close to the river until he reached the jungle which was supposed to camouflage the entrance to the tunnel, then he had to strike off right, and skirt round it. It was many years since Miss Adeline had played here with her brother Maurice, and gone down into the tunnel. What might then have been little saplings, or plants seeded by the wind or by birds, would have had time to grow up and mature, even to die. She had lived a very long life.

As he rounded the end of the untidy plantation and made his way back towards the river path, he noticed that the Abbey buildings were actually much nearer than they had realised. It was certainly possible that a tunnel to the river *had* been dug, starting in a corner of an outlying cellar.

It reminded him of the true story of *The Wooden Horse* which described how, during World War Two, some English prisoners had escaped from a German camp by digging a tunnel out from the middle. They had used a wooden vaulting horse with a false bottom, to hide in while they were digging. It had always seemed such a fantastic tale to him, but it was absolutely true, and the men had escaped – unlike this pathetic-sounding boy called William Neale. If he had ever existed at all, which Sam still doubted.

As he shifted the cat basket in his arms Arthur mewed rather piteously, and two boys sitting by the river with fishing rods looked round. 'Be quiet, Arthur, it's OK,' he whispered. Then, to the boys, 'sorry'. Fishing bored him, but his father liked it, and he knew it was important to move about quietly and not to disturb the fish.

'It's OK,' said one of them casually, opening an old tobacco tin, the kind beloved of Sam's father, the kind which would contain important mysteries to do with flies and maggots. 'Not much doing round here. Fish gone on holiday, strikes me.'

Sam walked slowly past and saw, sitting on a fallen tree trunk, perhaps on one of the stricken elms, an old woman who was watching the boys intently. She was thin and, in spite of the stifling heat, was muffled up in black. Her skirt came down to her ankles. She looked like an ancient widow woman, the kind of old crone he'd seen last year when he'd gone on the school trip to Greece.

Arthur was not happy inside his wicker prison, in fact he now seemed rather disturbed. He had started howling, and chewing at the bars of the tiny window cut out of the front of the basket, desperate to get out. His howling was that of a very frightened animal, hopelessly trapped. Sam didn't like it. It felt cruel, keeping him imprisoned like this. He must get back to the Abbey. 'Hello,' he called out, as he walked past the hunched-up figure sitting on the fallen tree. What was this ancient lady doing here, watching two boys fish by a quiet river?

At the sound of Sam's voice, she got slowly to her feet and he saw that she was very tall and very slender. Her hair was plentiful for one so old and carefully and elaborately braided, as if she had just stepped out of some expensive *salon*. Where it was not grey it was the faint colour of strawberries and this told him it must have once been red, like his Aunt Helen's hair.

Sam stopped in the path and something made him say, 'Can I help you?' Immediately, the old woman turned her face to him and their eyes met. She saw a freckled, hot young face and a tangle of coarse dark hair dusted with fine thistledown that had drifted across the water. He saw an ancient lined countenance, with deep channels carved into the sides of the mouth and more channels defining the nose, and there were deep furrows seaming the forehead. It was a good strong face which might once have been beautiful, but it was the saddest he had ever seen.

Her eyes, a bright hard blue, now searched his face, but he saw that there was no recognition in them. He felt she had been expecting some other person and that he had come instead and was a disappointment. The kitten now howled very loudly and started to spit, managing to jam its head in the window in the wicker-basket, in its efforts to escape. The old woman had already turned away and was walking along the river bank, past the two boys hunched over their rods, walking very upright, almost stalking, holding up her long dress with thin white hands. And as Sam watched her go a chill swept across him, the sudden chill of a still, hot day when different weather is coming, heralded by peevish gusts of wind.

All the way back to the Abbey, he talked to Arthur through the wicker bars, comforting him, promising instant release and a handful of the crunchy cat biscuits that he loved. But all he could think about was the lean black figure and the beautiful, anguished face which remained imprinted on his memory, long after the grey-green beauty of the river and its trees had faded.

XII

Next morning, Magnus, who had slept very badly, woke once again at precisely twenty-past five. It was as if there was an alarm clock inside his head. At bedtime, Sam had talked of coming with him to the swimming pool, but Magnus had been vague about his plans. He couldn't cope with Sam, who'd won medals for swimming, tearing up and down the pool while he did his pathetic hopping performance, clinging on to the sides. His plan was to go to the pool on his own each morning, and practise. That way he'd be swimming properly by the end of the holiday.

Fortunately, Floss and Sam were sleeping soundly. They'd all sat up late last night, discussing how they could get into the middle of that overgrown shrubbery where the tunnel entrance was. Sam had had a look in Wilf's workshop, with its orderly array of all kinds of tools, and Cousin Maude had plenty of gardening implements too, hung on pegs in her greenhouse. But they couldn't just help themselves. Expensive tools that went missing would attract immediate attention. If they borrowed them officially, however, they would have to explain what they were needed for, and that meant taking Wilf, and possibly Cousin Maude, into their confidence.

Sam had not told the others about the old woman on the river bank. He wished he hadn't seen her and he wished he could stop thinking about her. He was trying to persuade himself that she was just a vague, lost old woman from the village, but he knew that this was not true. The Lady Alice Neale had appeared to him, but as an old lady, and it was not Sam she had wanted to see. When their eyes met she had immediately turned away.

Magnus pondered on the question of the tools as he pulled on his swimming trunks. Colonel Stickley had obligingly stayed in London for the rest of the week and yesterday, Cousin Maude had talked about going to a national garden show on the other side of Birmingham. So perhaps it was only Wilf they'd have to deal with – or deceive. The problem was, they all liked him so much. The thought of lying to Wilf did not appeal.

Before he crept away, Magnus checked his tell-tale piece of sticking plaster inside the fireplace. His heart came up into his throat when he saw it. The plaster had most definitely stretched and it was now strained quite tautly across the two broken lips of wall. They had moved apart, even though the movement was infinitesimal.

He took his clasp knife and made a tiny nick in the top of the sticking plaster – it had a plastic coating and wouldn't tear very easily on its own. This cut might help the process, unless of course the plaster itself came off the wall. He noted down what he'd done in his "Appearances" notebook and dated the entry. If the workmen turned up today, and started disturbing things at the base of the turret, it would be interesting to see what happened to this piece of plaster.

Arthur appeared as he stepped out of the front door and scampered along beside him as far as the outer door of the pool, which was again propped open, though there was no sign of Wilf. Could this be a special act of kindness for the children alone? If so, Magnus was extremely grateful.

The little cat had stopped very suddenly at the door, almost skidding, as if brakes had been applied to his paws. Magnus picked him up and cuddled him, stroking his little round belly. 'You're getting too fat,' he whispered. 'You ought to eat less.' Then he carried him past the dusty pot plants and tried to show him the glinting blue water through the glass. But Arthur squirmed frantically, making the same throaty growling noise as yesterday. Then he leaped out of Magnus's arms and tore off in the direction of the Abbey.

When he was ready to swim, Magnus went into the pool area very cautiously. The cat had sensed something in this building. He had behaved just now in exactly the same way as on their first night, when the Lady Alice had walked out of her frame, when they had heard her weeping up in the turret room. Was she here again and was she actually waiting for him this time? Would she speak?

But nobody was there and he swam up and down, going over and over things in his mind. From the beginning, Arthur had been like a piece of litmus paper in the way he had reacted so sensitively to the various moods and feelings that were abroad in the Abbey. It was possible that, just now, he had picked up the presence of the Lady Alice Neale, even though Magnus could neither see her presence nor feel her nearness. Or was the cat's unease about something more ancient, and more general? Miss Adeline had told them yesterday that some of the old village people would not talk about this particular area of the Abbey estate. It had always been called The Field and it was rumoured to be an ancient burial place. They hadn't wanted Colonel Stickley to disturb it in order to build a swimming pool, but he had ignored them. The old lady hadn't said if anything had been found but, buried deep beneath this hideous twentieth-century construction, there might be the remains of hundreds of people. Or was it just one person? Was it the skeleton of William Neale, and was that why his mother had appeared to Magnus, here?

When he got back, the other two were up, washed and dressed. Magnus expected recriminations from Sam for not having waited for him, but the other boy made no comment. He was much too preoccupied with the problem of getting the necessary tools for their assault on the shrubbery.

'I know it's hot but I think you should put jeans on today,' he told Magnus. Both he and Floss were wearing theirs. 'We're going to get scratched to bits, trying to get into the centre of those bushes. And take something with long sleeves to put on, you'll need to protect your arms.'

Eventually, feeling sweaty and over-dressed, they trooped down the cool stone spiral of steps to join Cousin M for breakfast in the Great Hall. But she wasn't there. A sheet of paper stuck to the cereal box explained, in her big, generous handwriting, that she had set off early for the garden show near Birmingham, to try and avoid traffic jams on the M6, and that she might stay overnight with a friend. Wilf would be around all day and they could have the run of the Abbey. 'Heaps of love,' it ended.

Propped against the box were three postcards from Majorca, from their parents, one for each of them; some stone steps at the end of a flower-hung alley, a stunning blue sea ringed with mountains, a simple white church. Magnus looked at his for a long time and before setting off with the others to talk to Wilf, went upstairs and slid it under his pillow. Cousin M was mothering him and he liked her a lot but he still had moments of missing his foster parents, especially the children's mother, who was always so kind to him and whom he allowed, privately, to hug him. She would have understood why the story of the tormented William Neale had distressed him so much and he thought too that she might have understood why, now, it felt so vital to find out what had happened to him, and why they were going down the tunnel. But if William *was* buried underneath the swimming pool building, how could anybody get him out? The ghost would be grieving for ever, it seemed to him.

Wilf, who was all set to go off in *Salut d'Amour* for a few hours fishing, didn't actually ask them why they wanted to borrow a spade, a saw, a couple of hammers and a jemmy. Sam's vague opening gambit had been that they wanted to do some exploring in the grounds.

Having shown them where he kept his tools, Wilf said very casually, 'I suppose it's that old passage under the water you're after, is it? Miss A tell you all about it, did she? Don't get too excited. I've never been able to find it myself. Have fun.'

Somewhat crushed by this they set off for the river, carrying the tools between them. They'd gone into Maude's greenhouse on the way and they now had a pair of secateurs each. Sam seemed to think the initial assault would involve cutting away a lot of upper branches, otherwise they wouldn't actually be able to see where they were going at ground level. Before they began, Sam got himself high enough in a big tree to be able to look down and site the remains of the elms by the river, and from these he worked out a rough line back, to where the shrubbery ended.

He decided that they should start by cutting a passage about half a metre wide, from the land side of the shrubbery into the middle, and they set to work with their secateurs, cutting through the thicker branches with the saw. It was back-breaking work and they were soon covered with scratches. Sam had been right to insist on long sleeves, on jeans and thick socks.

Once they'd made a bit of headway they discovered that it wasn't so daunting as they'd imagined, that in a funny way it was quite satisfying. You could sometimes advance several metres over sweet-smelling peaty soil where nothing at all grew, and some of the little bushes could be pushed aside, or stepped over. Only when it was something thick and dense did the hacking become necessary.

They worked hard and in virtual silence for nearly two hours and then found, to their general dismay, that they had actually reached the river. 'Oh,' said Floss, 'we've done it, we've come right through the shrubbery. Now what do we do?'

'Would anyone like some of this?' Magnus said, wiping his forehead. 'I feel dehydrated. Wilf gave me this flask. I think it's iced lemonade,' and he handed it to Floss.

'Brilliant,' she said, taking a long swig. Her throat was parched. 'Want some, Sam?' she said. 'It's really cold.'

But Sam was staring across the water at the thin black figure he'd seen yesterday. She was sitting on the bank staring straight at him. He hesitated, then waved aimlessly. 'Hello,' he called. 'Hot again, isn't it?' But the old woman did not reply, merely got to her feet and began to walk away in the direction of the village.

His eyes followed her until she was lost in the trees then, very slowly, he turned back to the others. Magnus had not seen the old woman because, after swigging the lemonade, he'd disappeared into the bushes for a minute, 'to attend to himself', which was how Father Godless had always described answering a call of nature, and Floss was still there. If Magnus had been with him at that moment, would the old woman have stayed? Might she even have glided across the river as she had glided across the swimming pool, and spoken to him? Sam felt cold again, but he decided the cold was coming from inside himself, and was the cold of fear, until a sharp gust rippled the water, turning it momentarily into choppy little ocean waves.

Magnus was now staring glumly at the great flat discs which marked the place where the diseased elms had been sheered away. 'She said holly trees,' he reminded them, 'and we didn't see a single holly in there, you know. There was hawthorn and there were brambles but definitely no holly. I think we're on quite the wrong track.' And he sat down to examine his scratches.

'Thanks for your support,' Sam replied sarcastically. 'I don't agree, and I'll show you why.' He turned away from them, knelt down and wormed his way back through the passage they had cleared until he reached the massive copper beech from which he had taken his bearings. Then he clambered up it until he had an overview of the shrubbery, and of the river and the fields beyond. Then, from his jeans pocket, he produced the small compact pair of binoculars his father took to cricket matches, put them to his eyes and swept the landscape.

First, he trained them on the thick shrubbery, locating Floss and Magnus on the river bank, dangling their feet in the water. From up here, he could see that to the left of the passage they had hacked out there seemed to be quite a big area, where nothing much grew. This formed a rough square and in one corner of it were the dark glossy tops of what looked to him like holly. This, perhaps, was the bit they should explore next. Sam wasn't giving up yet. He was quite enjoying this safari, it appealed to his practical nature. But now he shared Magnus's reason for wanting to uncover the tunnel. The ghost had appeared to him, even to *him*, who had not believed. He should tell the others. But not yet.

He was about to make his way down again when he realised that from here he might get a view of the village. He climbed higher, to the next fork. Then he trained the binoculars on the terrain that lay to his right, first picking out the sinuous river, then the red roofs of the village, then the church spire. He could see the black dot of the old woman who, having emerged from a fuzz of trees, was moving along a whitish track that led from the water on to a hooped stone bridge over which, as he stared, a red van slowly passed.

Floss said, when he joined them again, 'Find anything?'

He was cautious. 'Well, there are some holly trees nearer to the middle, and what looks like some waste ground. It might be worth trying there. But if you want to go back—'

'No. But could we have a rest? I'd quite like to swim in the pool Cousin Maude showed us. If I don't, I'm going to melt.'

'I'll come,' Magnus said. 'I'm not swimming, though. I might just… paddle.'

Sam said, 'OK'. The plan suited him. 'See you in a bit, then. I'm going to the village for another mosey round.' And he set off briskly along the river path. Something felt urgent suddenly. He wanted to talk to that old woman.

When he reached the bridge, he was held up by a queue of traffic. The road across it was too narrow for two cars to pass and there was a line of waiting vehicles and a policeman in a car, monitoring the flow. Sam didn't dare dodge dangerously across. He had to wait for a gap.

As he stood there, he saw the old woman enter the church. By the time he had reached it and gone inside there was no sign of her. The only other occupant of the airy, simple building was the officious middle-aged man who had spoken to him last time, and shown him the guide book, a neatly-suited individual with small gold spectacles, who eyed Sam up and down just as he'd done before, as if people only came into churches to steal things.

Sam wandered round, enjoying the coolness and the play of branches against the plain, uncoloured glass in the square Tudor windows, breathing in a sweet mustiness from the undecorated pews. The elaborate Neale memorial, so highly painted, looked like a fairground object in the midst of so much understated simplicity. He looked again at all the Latin writing and wished he could translate. Only one thing seemed to be in English and this appeared several times, painted on scrolls set underneath several of the pious effigies of people at prayer: *Perfecte love casteth out feare*.

He looked round for the old woman, peering into side chapels and then behind a blue felt curtain where bell-ropes hung, and vestments, and old brooms. She was definitely not there, so he turned to go out again. As he walked towards the great west door, his eyes travelled up to a wooden gallery which he hadn't noticed last time, a simple structure, the same unadorned oak as the pews, which must once have held musicians. In the middle of this gallery stood the old lady. She was staring down at him, staring straight into his eyes and with one long thin hand, heavily ringed he noticed, she was pointing to the Neale memorial.

The face of the modern boy stared up into the face of the Elizabethan widow. It was an ancient face, a face cut almost to pieces by its channels of pain, and of grief, but it was the face he had seen before in the painting, when it was a younger, harder face, before all this life had happened to it.

'You are looking at an authentic minstrels' gallery, young man,' said a voice behind him. The officious caretaker, wearing a brass badge that said 'Robert Atherton, Sidesperson', was standing at his elbow. 'Read your Thomas Hardy? Read *Under the Greenwood Tree*? That's the kind of gallery they'd have played in, with their fiddles and such like. I prefer a good organ myself.'

Sam turned round when the man spoke to him but almost immediately looked back again, up into the gallery. In that instant, the figure in black had disappeared totally. He looked back wildly, and in some anguish, at Robert Atherton. 'Can I – ca – ca – can I go up?' he stammered, his heart thumping violently. 'It's, I'm, I'm very keen on history. I'd like to see it properly.'

But the man folded his arms across his chest with a definite satisfaction. 'I'm afraid not. The stairs became dangerous and they had to be removed.'

Something in Sam hardened. The man was obviously lying. 'But I've just seen someone, someone up there,' he said. 'She was there a few seconds ago.'

'Oh really? When?'

'I've told you, *just now*. It was quite an old woman. She was definitely there.'

The man glanced at his wristwatch. 'As I say, young man, they removed the stairs several years ago. There is no way of getting up there these days. Now, if you don't mind, I have to lock up for an hour. It's my lunch time. We don't leave the church unattended any more, there's too much vandalism. And he began to steer Sam towards the door.

But Sam shook him off. 'Listen,' he said hotly, 'there *are* stairs, they're behind that door, aren't they?' For not only had he seen the old woman up in the gallery, he had seen a pencil-slim bulge in a side wall which obviously concealed a spiral staircase which led up to it. This man was lying.

Robert Atherton sighed indulgently and produced a large bunch of keys. 'Well,' he said, 'you certainly know your church architecture, and you're right, the stairs were there, originally. But as I explained, they were removed years ago. Let me put your mind at rest. Come on.'

He unlocked the tiny timbered door, pulled it open and allowed Sam to go before him into a small round room. And when he looked very carefully, Sam realised that he had told the truth. Visible on the walls were dark lines indicating the former existence of a spiral staircase. But it was there no longer, and the roof of the chamber came down so low that Sam could almost touch it with his hands.

XIII

All through the afternoon, they worked away in the shrubbery. The patch of waste ground, and the holly trees which Sam thought he had seen from the tree, were much further away from the passage they had cleared than he'd thought. Magnus began to grumble. 'Are you *sure* this is right?' he said. 'We seem to be getting into thicker and thicker stuff, to me. Something's biting me too. We'll have to go back, I can't stand much more of this.'

Sam took no notice but hacked away in silence. He was locked in his own world, still thinking of what had happened in the church, and of what they might find in this tunnel, should they ever uncover an entrance. The face staring down at him from the gallery was unmistakeably the face of Lady Alice Neale. No-one would easily forget its strong, hard lines, its austere beauty, unyielding, even in the teeth of time. He had seen his first ghost. Did ghosts, therefore, grow old? And did they really try to communicate and change the course of history? He'd thought their lives existed parallel to one's own but this ghost seemed to want something from them, or rather, from Magnus. Magnus was certainly the key to it.

Sam felt he was in very deep waters, plunged into them against his will and into something to do with time and suffering and regret that he did not begin to understand. But the incident in the church had definitely happened. He had seen the Lady Alice for himself now, like Doubting Thomas who also would not believe until he had hard evidence. But what was he to do with this evidence? He must tell the other two but then he would feel foolish because, all along, he had been so scornful. Nobody liked admitting they were wrong.

Magnus suddenly announced that the midges were eating him alive. 'It's because we've come back to the river,' said Floss, trying to be helpful. 'I suppose they could be mosquitoes.'

'Oh *no*!' Magnus said dramatically. 'We could get malaria, people *can* get it here, you don't have to go to India to catch malaria.'

But Floss had had enough. 'For heaven's sake, Mags,' she said, 'don't be such a wimp.'

But then Sam called out, 'Shut up, just SHUT UP, the pair of you,' and they saw him drop down on to his knees, and begin to wriggle under a low bush. They watched as he slowly disappeared from sight then a silence fell. At first there was only the gentle movement of tree branches, the occasional bird and a plop as something moved on the river. Then they heard Sam's voice, shrill with excitement, 'I've found it, honestly, I really have! And it's not even covered over with earth, let alone with a bush or anything. This is fantastic!'

'We're coming!' Magnus shouted, and he plunged into the undergrowth in the direction of Sam's voice, not even bothering to wriggle through, but staying upright, fighting his way through the trees. Floss followed and within seconds they had found the tiny clearing where Sam stood, blood trickling down one cheek from a deep scratch and a bruise on the other.

He was standing with folded arms looking down and grinning. 'That's what we're looking for,' he said, kicking at something. 'And I can see where we went wrong. There were more elms here, look, you can see where they cut them down. But they're further along, and not right on the river, like the others. I suppose Cousin M didn't think of that.'

Magnus dropped on to his knees and started brushing leaf mould off whatever it was that Sam was kicking with his foot. Floss joined him and soon they found themselves looking at a square metal plate, roughly a metre square. Very slowly, together, the three of them brought their faces very close to the ground, and looked. There was a moment of silence then Magnus said in disgust 'It says "Harrington, Stoke on Trent". It's a *manhole cover*, that's all it is.'

But Sam shoved Magnus aside quite roughly. 'I know what it is, Magnus. There are lots of them around. But the point is, what's it doing here in the middle of a wood? They could easily have used a drain cover, to hide the tunnel entrance. They'd have done it on purpose.'

'It reminds me of that lamp post in the middle of Narnia,' Floss said dreamily. Because Sam was obviously furious with Magnus, she didn't say that she too felt disappointed because the cover probably concealed no more than a boring old drain. She said, trying to sound encouraging, 'Miss Adeline would have been a little girl in the nineteen hundreds, wouldn't she? Surely they had drain covers by then?'

'They did,' Magnus informed her. 'Victorian sewers are marvellous. Where I used to live, in Deptford—'

But Sam interrupted. This wasn't the moment for a lecture on sewers. 'We need the spade,' he said, 'and the jemmy Wilf gave us. Come on. We won't shift it in five minutes, not after the time it's been sitting here.'

The first thing they did was the most obvious, which was to take turns in pulling on the iron ring in the middle. But the plate was immoveable. From his backpack, Magnus silently produced a small coil of rope. Sam, looping it round the ring, was impressed. 'What made you bring that, Mags?' he asked.

Magnus shrugged. 'Dunno. Thought a rope might come in useful. I've brought one or two more things, as well. But let's see if this works first.'

They knotted the rope firmly to the ring, took hold of it and pulled. Nothing at all happened at first, then there was a clinking sound. The rope gave suddenly, and sent them tottering backwards. Eagerly they rushed forward, to inspect the cover.

But it hadn't moved. Instead, the iron ring had crumbled away into rusty red lumps.

'Time to try the key, don't you think, Mags?' Sam said, in a respectful voice. He was impressed by the provision of the rope. He took it from his pocket and unwrapped the tissue paper. It was a thick heavy key, very plain and business-like, of a dull grey clean metal and with not a spot of rust. It looked as if Miss Adeline might have polished it regularly.

'Let's spray a bit of this in the hole first,' said Magnus, rummaging in his backpack and producing a blue aerosol can. 'This loosens rusty locks and things. We can put a bit on the key as well.'

'Brilliant,' Floss said, putting a hand on his shoulder and staring down at 'Harrington, Stoke on Trent.' She was still finding it hard to believe that there was anything more than a drain underneath the cover, but the two boys were now tense and silent.

Sam inserted the key and turned gently, first to the left, then to the right. 'No go,' he said. 'I don't want to break anything inside the lock. You have a try, Mags.'

Magnus squatted beside him and fiddled with the key for a long time, stopping now and again to squirt in more of the de-rusting agent. After some minutes they heard a dull clunking noise and Magnus's back stiffened. He stood upright and wiped his forehead. 'Done it. I've definitely turned the key in the lock. But now what do we do?'

'Let's try levering it up with the jemmy,' Sam suggested. So they inserted the flat end under the edge of the manhole cover. Then Sam stood on the main part of the handle, leaning all his weight upon it. 'Please be careful,' Floss said anxiously. 'If the blade snaps it could go in someone's eye.' But Sam, who seemed to be growing increasingly frantic in their efforts to dislodge the infuriating cover, jumped up and down on the twanging blade. Magnus and Floss retreated. 'You're moving it,' Magnus said in excitement, 'so it's definitely unlocked. But I think we'll have to dig round the sides a bit. Good job the earth's fairly soft.'

Sam picked up the spade and began to jab round the edges of the cover with the blade. 'Mags,' he said humbly. 'You didn't by any chance bring a torch, did you?'

'Yes, I did, I brought one each. There were two in Wilf's shed.' His was the army one that had belonged to Father Godless, the one he kept by him at night, in case something frightened him. Its little pencil beam wouldn't do much to penetrate the kind of darkness they might encounter under the river.

Sam had already started digging seriously round all four sides of the manhole cover. There was only one spade so the others watched. Quite soon the soft earth started to fall away, as there began to be an indentation of several centimetres all round it. 'Mind where you put your feet,' warned Sam, 'the whole thing might cave in.' But before anybody actually jumped clear, they saw a sizeable hole appear, gaping blackly between 'Harrington, Stoke on Trent' and their neat ridges of sweet-smelling forest floor. Silently, as if under orders from some unseen leader, each took hold of a corner of the metal cover, lifted it away quite easily and set it on the ground. Then they looked down.

They saw a flight of very narrow steps disappearing into blackness and curved, rough walls lined with stones and pieces of flint. A dank, sour smell came up at them and Sam, touching the rocky walls, withdrew his hand sharply. 'Ugh, it's slimy.'

'Well, it's bound to be,' said Magnus in a flat, matter-of-fact voice. 'It goes under a river. Come on then, there's a torch each. And he handed Sam a big yellow flashlight, and Floss a stout rubber torch, keeping Father Godless's little green one for himself. 'I'll go at the back,' he said.

Sam, at the front, did not budge. 'Come *on*!' Magnus said irritably, 'or do you want me to lead?'

'No. No, it's OK. Only… it's terribly narrow. Hope we don't get stuck. I – you all right, Floss? Do you want to stay out here?'

'No.' she snapped. 'Do you?' Without another word, and not understanding himself what he was so afraid of, Sam put his foot gingerly on the first of the slimy steps and went down into the darkness.

XIV

They realised afterwards, when they swam across the river from bank to bank, that they could have only advanced a few yards through the tunnel, but now, while they were deep inside it, and inching blindly forwards through the foul darkness, it felt as if it must be miles long. The roof of it scraped their heads and the sides were so close that at times even Magnus, who was terribly thin, had to turn sideways to get through. In one place they had to crouch and wriggle under a spar of timber that had fallen from the roof. When they shone their torch beams upwards, they could see that it was a properly constructed tunnel, the walls lined with lumps of knobbled flint mixed with river stones and the odd brick, all crudely plastered together and shored up with timbers which, amazingly, had not rotted away. Underfoot, they were squelching through what felt like thick mud.

Nobody spoke. All three knew instinctively that all any of them wanted was for the tunnel to end, in daylight, in a blank wall, anything – just as long as they could legitimately turn round and go back. Floss was starting to panic. She had always loathed stuffy enclosed spaces and she tried to avoid going in lifts or up into lofts or in things like ghost trains at a funfair. The fear she hoped she might have conquered was now coming back. It was rising up into her mouth, and it was getting very big. It was threatening to become a scream.

But then, just as she thought she really would have to go back, she heard Sam call out, 'Hey, it's widening out. It's a kind of room.' And soon they were all standing together in the middle of a rough-walled chamber, with a domed roof, the top-most point of which was considerably higher than the tunnel.

Although there was now plenty of space around them they stood in a little knot, their bodies touching for reassurance, looking round them. 'It's empty,' Magnus said in a small voice. 'I thought—
' 'What?' Sam's voice too sounded crest-fallen. 'Did you expect – human remains? The remains of the boy?'

'Of course not, though I suppose they might be in a cavity, say, under the floor. We might have to dig.'

Floss shivered. It just sounded too horrible, too like hideous murders one saw on the TV news. The police were always digging for people. She said 'We can't do that, Mags.'

'Why not? The mother wants her son. She wants him to be decently buried. That's what we're here for.'

'I'll go back if you start digging,' she said.

'On your own?'

'Yes, if I have to.'

'Listen. Just wait a minute.' Sam was running the beam of his torch all over the chamber. The floor was made of brick and against one wall a slab of stone had been placed across two smaller stone supports, to make a bench. More slabs of stone, looking like the ruins of a table, lay on the floor, but apart from these things the room really was empty. Directly opposite where they had stepped out of their tunnel, another tunnel began, but they could see from where they stood that it was impassable. It only went in about a foot before ending abruptly in a wall of flints and bricks, all firmly mortared into place, with two great beams driven into the ground to shore the wall up, in the shape of an 'X'.

Sam said 'Perhaps they never took the tunnel as far as the other side of the river. It looks as if they gave up. This must have just been a hiding place. After all, you could have taken a boat across the river I suppose, under cover of darkness.'

Magnus was now working his way systematically round the walls of the chamber with his torch, but Floss's fear of dark, enclosed spaces was creeping over her again. 'Look, you can see that there's nothing here,' she said. '*Please* can we go back?' It was enough that she had braved the darkness and come this far. Now she wanted to return to the river and sit in the sun.

'I'm looking for something,' he said. 'Not a body. But Miss Adeline told us that her brother used to hide his treasures here. Remember? There's got to be a little hidey-hole. But where?'

'In the walls, perhaps?' Sam suggested, flashing his big yellow light up and down. But the crude mixture of brick and flint was firmly cemented together. Between them they went over every inch, but there was no loose stone that pulled out, revealing a hiding place.

Next they turned their attention to the brick floor which was raised higher than the floor of the tunnel which was mainly mud mixed with small river stones. The floor of the chamber itself was perfectly dry. Care had obviously been taken in the construction of this little room, presumably built to shelter people who might have had to stay in hiding for weeks. When he could find no obvious place where bricks had been removed, then replaced, Sam squatted down to look at the floor more closely. But Floss, who was now back inside the tunnel, noticed that Magnus too was standing at a distance, viewing the floor as a whole. For a minute or two he said nothing, then he seemed to pounce. 'That's the place,' he said. 'That's got to be it.'

'Why?' demanded Sam. 'That's the one damp bit. No point in hiding anything there.'

'But that's exactly it! It's damp because there's cold air trapped underneath it, so there must be a space. Manholes are always the last things to dry, for the same reason. I bet that's it. Come *on*… good thing I brought this.'

But Sam was sceptical and Floss, who could feel her panic rising, was increasingly desperate to get away. They stood side-by-side, watching as Magnus drove the blade of the chisel into the joints between the damp bricks, working it carefully round each one. Then they saw that he was lifting them out, and placing them beside him in an orderly pile. They crept closer. Floss found that Sam was holding her hand. She gave his fingers a reassuring squeeze because he was shaking as much as she was. Magnus was lifting something out of the hole in the floor.

It was quite large and wrapped in brownish cloth that smelt as if it had been impregnated with oil. Magnus handed this over to Sam who, instinctively, folded it up carefully and placed it on top of the bricks. Then they looked at the box which he was holding up in front of him with the air of one of the Three Wise Men. 'Well, I know what that is,' Floss said. 'It's an old travelling writing desk. Aunt Helen's got one. She's leaving it to Sam in her will.'

Magnus placed the box on the floor and they all

looked at it. The oily cloth had preserved the beautifully figured wood from which it was made, but had blackened the brass plate set into the lid. On this, barely visible, engraved in thin, flowing letters, was the name 'Maurice Scott-Carr'. 'That's Miss Adeline's surname too,' Floss said. 'It's on a little notice next to her front door. Open it, Mags.'

'I don't know if I can,' he said, his voice steely with tension. 'It's got a keyhole too. It might be locked.'

But as they watched they saw him open the box quite easily. The inside of the lid divided into two halves, each fitting together to make the small leathered slope of a writing desk. Set into the top were two small bottles of ink, and a polished ledge for pens. 'It's *just* like Aunt Helen's,' Floss said. 'You pull that bit of ribbon and there's space to store things, underneath.'

'I *know*,' said Magnus, and he opened up the storage space to reveal a small package, wrapped in the same kind of oily cloth which had protected the box. Carefully he unwrapped it, took out a bundle of yellowish papers tied round with string, and held them in his hands. He was breathing very fast in the silence.

'What are they, do you think?' Sam said. Magnus had handled everything with such reverential care he didn't dare rush him now.

'I'm not sure. They look like little books. Look,

it's a lot of sections sewn together. But there aren't any covers. 'Of course, nowadays they'd be glued – that's why books fall apart – but these have been sewn together, with silk I think.'

'The string's rotten,' warned Sam. 'It'll disintegrate if we try to undo it.'

'I don't think we should,' Floss said, 'at least, not yet. This all belongs to Miss Adeline. Shouldn't we take it to her first?'

But Magnus was already teasing out something from under the string, a folded piece of paper which looked rather newer than the little silk bound bundles. He opened it and it separated into two pieces, so he pieced the two halves together and held them up in front of his face. 'Can you shine your torches,' he said. 'There's some writing on this. It's a bit faded.'

But he found that even in the wavering light he could read what was written quite easily, because it was in a bold round hand, honest, unpretentious writing, the hand of a boy like Sam, perhaps, who liked climbing trees and being practical.

Magnus read, first to himself and then aloud:

'"The only known evidence of the existence of the unfortunate William Neale, whose grieving mother is supposed to haunt the Abbey, was uncovered in the 1850s by some workmen repairing a floor. Taking up the boards they came across some papers mixed up with rubble. On examination these proved to be copy books, such as a schoolboy might use, of the Tudor period. Corrections had been made on many of them, in a hand that was identified from other manuscripts, as that of the Lady Alice Neale. Each book was signed 'William, His Booke,' and, significantly, nearly every page of them was badly blotched.' (taken from my father's, Edmund Scott-Carr's, unpublished *History of the Abbey*)'"

'Go on,' said Floss. 'What else does it say?'

'That's it. There isn't any more. Maurice must have copied it out of something his father was writing. Perhaps Miss Adeline's got it.'

'But I wonder why he took the books,' Sam said, 'and hid them here?'

'He was going to the war,' Floss said, 'and his own father was dead. Miss Adeline told us that. Maurice had already inherited the Abbey. But he knew he might never come back, and he didn't. He was killed. He didn't know what was going to happen to the Abbey, it could have been sold off, anything. I think he put them here to keep them safe. Only his sister knew where he'd put his treasures.'

Sam was fingering the ancient little books, under the string. 'Look, it says "William, His Booke"',' he said in wonder. 'Look, on the very first page of the very first one. And someone *has* corrected it. They've written over the top.'

Everything was in Latin but it was obvious that a grown up had stood over the boy, ferociously crossing out his own pathetic scribblings.

'Poor William, he really was messy,' Floss murmured. 'Look at all those blots.'

But Magnus said very sadly, 'They look more like tears to me.'

XV

With Magnus holding Edmund Scott-Carr's Victorian writing box, and its cache of ancient copy books blotted by little William Neale, they made their way back through the tunnel, up the steps and out into the dappled sunlight of the trees. Nobody said very much. Together they pulled the manhole cover back into place and scattered leaf mould over it, to hide their traces. They were all thinking about Miss Adeline, and about what she might say when she saw the box. 'You will know what you are looking for, when you have found it, she had told them.

The copy books were proof William Neale existed, unless of course they were fakes. But that was not the whole of the story, nor the end of it. What had really happened? And where was his body?

As they walked away from the river they were all thinking about the cruelty meted out to William Neale. Sam felt very much at one with him because he himself never did brilliantly at school, and a teacher had once called him thick. Floss was wondering more about William's mother and father. She herself had a hot temper, like Lady Alice, and she could quite see how you could lash out and hit someone just a little bit too hard, with the most horrible consequences. If that had happened, then she felt sorry for Lady Alice Neale.

Magnus could think only of William, subject to cruel torments for nothing that was his fault, subject to impossible pressures, being driven to learn so that he could achieve and achieve, being confined in a tiny room, somewhere even smaller than the chamber under the river, shut up and accidentally left to die. His own father had driven him hard, when he'd been tutoring him, and had lost his temper when Magnus had got things wrong. He'd hit him sometimes and called him an idiot. In the end, he'd become very strange and withdrawn, then he'd simply walked out of the house and left them. They never saw him again, though he sent money sometimes, in brown envelopes, so they knew he was still alive. That was when Magnus's mother had become ill in her mind. Not knowing what she was doing, she had carried on his father's cruelty, and shut him up, and made him do housework and not let him go out to play.

When they got to Miss Adeline's cottage, they were ready to use the knocker at least three times, but the door was opened after the first knock, not by Miss Adeline, but by a large middle-aged woman in a pink nylon overall. She was holding a duster.

'We've come to see Miss Adeline,' Magnus said. 'We're from the Abbey. We're staying with Maude, and Colonel Stickley.'

'Are you now?' said the woman, not very pleasantly and eyeing each of them in turn. 'Expecting you, was she?'

'Sort of,' Sam informed her, peering over her shoulder. But the woman came out on to the doorstep, blocking his view down the hall.

'She's not here. They took her into hospital this morning. She had a bit of a "turn", in the night. I just came in as usual to clean round, water her plants and that.'

Sam immediately thought about his godmother. 'It's not a stroke, is it?' he said anxiously.

The woman softened slightly. 'Not that I've heard, but she's more than ninety years old, you know. She's on borrowed time. "Past your sell-by date, Miss A," I tell her sometimes.'

'We'll come back when she's home,' Floss said.

'Want to leave that with me?' the woman said, looking inquisitively at the corner of the writing box which was poking out from its oil wrapping. 'That's hers, isn't it? Lent it to you, did she? My goodness, that's not like Miss A. She's very particular.'

'It's not hers,' Magnus, said, covering up the corner. 'Well, not exactly. It's something we've found that we wanted to show her.'

It was obvious that the cleaning woman did not quite believe him. 'Well, she's got something very like that,' she said suspiciously. 'It's for writing paper and stuff. It was her mother's, her name's on the lid.'

'Well, this was her *father's*,' said Magnus with great authority,' and we have to deliver it into her hands.'

Defeated, the woman made to shut the door. 'I'd watch yourselves today,' she said, as she watched them go down the path, 'if you're going back to the Abbey. There's been a bit of a do up there. Builders in trouble or something. They've done some damage, and they only made a start this morning. You can't trust anyone these days, to do a proper job. The Colonel's on his way back specially, from London. The police are up there now. I don't know. What with Miss A, and this heat, I need a sit-down. It never rains but it pours.'

'I know, it's awful isn't it,' Floss said sympathetically. It was obvious that the woman just wanted to talk; she was feeling a bit sorry for her. But the two boys hadn't even waited to hear the rest of the sentence. They'd already set off at a run towards the Abbey buildings, in spite of being impeded by all Wilf's tools and the writing box.

Floss caught up with them at the turn in the

drive. They could see several police cars, with engines running and blue lights flashing. Uniformed men were clustered round the base of the turret, pulling out long strings of luminous orange tape and sealing things off, in case people came too close.

Wilf was talking to one of the policemen, next to a builder's van, and someone was passing round a thermos flask. The three children looked at the turret. It seemed exactly as before, chubby, foursquare and reliable, apart from all the striped cones round it, and the festoons of waving plastic tape. 'What's happened, Wilf?' Sam shouted.

The man turned and waved. 'I don't know. Had a good day? Brought my tools back?' His face was quite blank, like a page upon which nothing at all would permit itself to be written. But Magnus was not deceived. 'What do you mean you "don't know", Wilf? Why are the police here?'

Before Wilf could open his mouth, a builder snorted, spraying tea all over his T-shirt. 'I'll tell you, sunny Jim, we've only gone and put a crack about a mile wide in the Colonel's precious tower.'

'But why are the *police* here?' persisted Magnus.

One of the officers came over to them and put a hand on Magnus's shoulder but the boy immediately shrank away. 'I'm afraid you can't go up to your room at the moment. We've had to seal it off. Your belongings have been brought down.

Look, they're over there. Mr Wilkinson tells me there's another place you can sleep.'

'My caravan,' said Wilf, 'the one in the stable yard. It's a snug little number, cosier than a portakabin. You don't want to go in one of those, you'll catch your death. Miss Maude'll sort it all out for you.'

'Isn't she still in Birmingham?' asked Sam.

'She was, but the Colonel telephoned her from London; she's on her way home. He's coming back too. He's had a piece of news, you see.' As he said this, a wave of emotion passed over Wilf's face, some strong feeling that seemed to the children to have come from his very core.

'What sort of news, Wilf?' asked Floss.

'Oh, y'know, just news,' and he swallowed very hard, and turned away.

The three children looked at each other and shrugged. Then Magnus said, 'Can't you tell us anything about the tower?'

Wilf looked at them. 'Well, one of the apprentices went mad with a drill, started work where he shouldn't have done, and it's caused a lot of damage. There's a crack down it now, from top to bottom, really big, you can almost get into it, and it's worst in your room, apparently.'

'Inside the fireplace?' asked Magnus.

'I can't say. Don't ask me. I've not been allowed up. They've sent for somebody from the Home Office now, they've obviously found something.'

'What?' said Magnus, thinking rapidly. Perhaps the Home Office person could have a look at the old copy books.

'I don't know. I haven't been told. That's the truth. That's because they've been waiting for the Colonel.'

'He's here,' Sam said. 'Well, someone's here.'

There was a chugging noise behind them, and a black London taxi came along the drive and stopped at the Abbey entrance. Colonel Stickley got out of it, spoke to somebody inside, noticed Wilf and the children, and came stalking across the grass, rapidly, with hardly a trace of the limp.

'What are the police doing here?' he said fiercely. 'I said no reporters, and they promised me faithfully—'

'Sir, they're here on other business,' Wilf said. 'There's been a discovery, up in one of the turret dormitories. Somebody's waiting to see you, to explain everything.'

But Colonel Stickley turned away. 'Can't see them just now, Wilf. It'll have to wait, whatever it is. Help me, will you… and these children.' He was staring down at them, blankly, as if he had never seen them before in his life. 'Could they carry things? I need a little help… in the taxi…'

'Hang on, sir,' said Wilf, taking a firm grip on the old man's arm. 'You're all knocked up.'

'It's David,' the old man said. 'He's in the taxi.'

Wilf stared at him. 'But sir, I thought they

couldn't fly him back until tomorrow. I was all set, little reception, the lot. There's no food laid on.'

'He doesn't want food, Wilf.' And the Colonel turned to the bewildered children. 'You see, it's my son. They released him and he's come home. He's in the taxi, my son David's in the taxi.' And he began to cry.

XVI

Rather shyly, Sam and Floss went forward to help, but Magnus withdrew and stood at some distance from the rest of them, under one of the great cedars that spread great shadows over the grass. This particular moment was too much for him, it was affecting him physically. There was a singing in his ears and he felt strangely light. He almost saw himself being plucked up from the lawn and borne away somewhere, into the summer sky. There was no longer a curse on the Abbey.

The son, who they had thought dead, had come home. Even as they had unwrapped the blotched copy books down in the tunnel, even as the wall of the turret had split, the living man, reunited with his father, had been coming home to the place that had been denied happiness for hundreds of years. Magnus was now quite certain that the Lady Alice would not walk again, or cry in the night. He believed that children would start coming back to the place. He believed that all would be well.

Wilf and Colonel Stickley were helping

someone out of the taxi. The policemen and the builders, who had obviously been told what had happened, all melted away discreetly. It was definitely not the time to ask about what had been discovered in the tower, nor to bring out the contents of the writing box. Floss took Magnus on one side and, trying to be very tactful, warned him to keep quiet for the time being. She knew that, once he had got his teeth into something, he was very reluctant to let it go. But he didn't need to be warned. He listened to the general talk and carried cases and thought about the time when he would be on his own again and able to do the thing which he had been brought to the Abbey to perform.

Cousin Maude got home minutes after the Colonel and everything became very emotional. Wilf cried and Maude cried, and David Stickley cried. Then everyone laughed. The Colonel brought up some bottles of wine from his cellar, and they all got slightly drunk. David Stickley, a thin, pale-faced man with the same gangling shape as his father, and with a shy, nice smile, said virtually nothing. He sat listening to the talk and stroking Arthur, who had curled up on his knee. When he was a child, he confided to Floss, he had wanted to be a vet. He hinted that Arthur was much too fat, which puzzled him because cats usually regulated their intake of food.

The three children listened hard to the talk about the man from the Home Office who was coming in the morning, but any mention of what the builders had found was extremely and deliberately vague. All Floss could think about was that wire coat hanger that had dropped into the crack. She had known all along that there was a space behind the fireplace.

It was fun going to bed in Wilf's caravan, but all Magnus wanted was for the other two to go to sleep. He had laid all his plans for the one thing left that he must do, for the one remaining piece of the puzzle that must now be fitted into place.

It was after midnight when he slipped out of the caravan and across the stable yard. In his pocket was a key to the main entrance of the Abbey. He had taken this from a cupboard fitted out to hold dozens of keys, which was concealed in an understairs closet off the Great Hall. Cousin Maude had trustingly shown them this, lest one of them should ever get locked in. In one hand he held Wilf's big yellow flashlight and in the other a carrier bag. This contained some of the dry cat biscuits that Arthur loved so much, and two pieces of raw steak which he'd taken from the freezer in the buttery.

The floodlights were still on and lit the arched entrance all too clearly. He opened the main door, slipped inside and closed it behind him. Then he shone the torch ahead of him and stepped forwards into the darkness.

A glimpse into the Great Hall showed him that the Lady Alice Neale was safely in her frame. At supper, they had talked about the Colonel's shipping the portrait to the USA for some great historic exhibition, in the spring. But did Colonel Stickley know what Miss Adeline had told them? That Lady Alice did not like to be moved, and about the night guard in the London gallery, who had actually asked to be relieved of his duties because the atmosphere in the room, where she had been temporarily hung, had turned icy cold, filling him with terror? That the guard, too, had found the great frame empty, in the middle of the night?

Magnus crept past the tapestry of Balaam and his donkey, thinking of the flop-eared beast bowing down before the angel, and of Arthur who had fled in fear from the presence of Lady Alice. He passed Pontius Pilate, for ever washing his guilt away, and crept down the chilly passageways until he reached the beginning of the stone spiral that led up to the turret dormitory. But here a dog rose to meet him. Magnus had the steak ready, and some of the cat biscuits, in case the dog didn't like the icy piece of meat. He scattered these liberally at the dog's feet and at once it sniffed inquisitively. Then it found the steak and, in spite of the ice crystals on it, started to attack it vigorously, with contented growly noises.

Magnus considered patting the dog, but decided it might suddenly remember what it had been posted there to do. So, giving it a wide berth and taking the second steak with him for the return journey, he began to ascend the stairs. The crack that ran down the inside of the turret had widened considerably, had become, in places, a jagged gaping hole, and he crunched over the debris of plaster and stones as he started to ascend.

The top room, their room, had a piece of orange tape stuck right across it and a sign that said No Entry. Very carefully, Magnus removed the tape, pushed open the door and went in. The room was quite bare now; the four divans and the flower-covered screens had been pushed against one wall. All the activity had obviously been focused on the fireplace, which was heavily criss-crossed with more orange tape. This too he removed and laid on the floor, hoping to be able to reconstruct it convincingly, for the police, before he went down again.

As he ducked his head and went under the canopy of the fireplace, he could feel his heart thumping. The drilling had had a devastating effect on this interior wall and there was a considerable heap of rubble roughly swept into one corner. He noticed his bit of sticking plaster on top of it. Now he was inside the fireplace, he could stand upright again. He shone the yellow torch on the hole that had appeared where the original thin crack had been. It was about half a metre across at its widest point and it ran from ceiling to floor. He was looking into a tiny little room, a mere cavity which had been made within the width of the thick turret wall.

The cavity was not empty, it was filled with bones, not random, scattered bones but with a complete, small skeleton. A child, still alive, or accidentally dead, must have been crammed into this tiny space. The knees were drawn up to rest where the chin would have been, and where now there was a grinning skull. The arms, every bone of them intact, still reached forwards and cradled the knees. Fingers, feet, ears, teeth, every bone of every part of the body was there, and in its proper place.

Magnus stepped back in horror. This was surely another 'Little Ease', that torment devised by torturers which he had seen on display in The London Dungeon, a tiny prison where the victim was similarly stuffed into the tiniest possible space, locked up, and left to die.

He hoped, with all his heart, that the child's body had been sealed here *after* death, by frightened servants, perhaps, desperate to conceal the truth from Lady Neale. Surely nobody would have devised this living death for a little child who could not learn his letters and who blotched his books? He stepped back from the cavity, stood quite still and closed his eyes. The pain of this was almost too much for one person to bear. He had become William Neale.

But he knew there was somebody else in the tower room with him as he suffered there, even though it was nobody he could see, and a feeling passed into him from that invisible presence, passed into him and gave him unexpected comfort, a feeling that was not fear but something more like grief.

XVII

Almost exactly a year later, Magnus went swimming on his own, at the hidden bathing place by the river. In the last twelve months he had practised whenever he could, and he'd won two certificates. He was confident now, and didn't at all mind going out of his depth, but he'd never had another chance to swim in a river pool. He'd been planning to do this ever since they'd known they were coming back to the Abbey. He regarded it as a private challenge.

That morning, there had been a ceremony down at the church to which the three children had been invited. The vault underneath the Neale memorial had been opened up and the child's skeleton buried inside it. The experts had told them that nobody would ever be able to say for certain who the child was, and whether or not he had been cruelly treated by his mother, or by both his parents, or indeed by persons unknown. He might have died by accident. No explanation was given at the ceremony and the child was not named. But

Colonel Stickley had wanted the anonymous bones laid to rest. Only then, he believed, would permanent peace come to the Abbey.

Miss Adeline, frail and more bird-like than ever, sat by the Colonel's side in the front pew, and next to her sat Magnus, Floss and Sam. None of the children doubted that they were saying goodbye at last to little William Neale, and neither did the old lady. In this very church Sam had seen the child's mother, in her old age, point to the Neale memorial, silently entreating him to perform this last office for her son. He had talked to Miss Adeline about it. She had a strong belief in God. She told him he had been granted this special meeting because, like the disciple Thomas, he had doubted most. She told them all that she had always known that the mother would walk in the Abbey until her little son was found and given his peace.

Magnus found that he missed the Lady Alice. It was as if the business between them was not quite finished. He wished he, and not Sam, had seen her up in the minstrels' gallery, because he believed she knew that he had suffered too, like her own son. That was why they had come to the Abbey in the first place, it wasn't mere coincidence.

Magnus had liked the simple service in the church and he'd thought old Father Godless would have approved of it too. David Stickley had read from the Bible and had quoted the Neale family motto: '*Perfect Love Casteth Out Fear.*' They had chosen this reading because, as Colonel Stickley explained to the congregation, far too many people had been afraid of the Lady Alice, both when she was alive and long after she was dead.

Magnus had become a special friend of David Stickley, mainly because of Arthur who, shortly after the three children had left for home, had given birth to a litter of kittens. David had been right about the kitten being 'too fat'. He'd looked after them and found people to take them. One of these was the children's mother. Their kitten was most definitely male, and gingery, like 'Mother' Arthur, who had broken all the rules, being a female marmalade cat. Cousin Maude, embarrassed at her mistake, had wanted to rename her Guinevere, after King Arthur's wife. But nobody wanted that, it was much too fussy a name and besides, Magnus had informed them that the real Guinevere had gone off with Sir Lancelot. So she remained "Mother Arthur", had more kittens and became very matronly.

It smelled sweet and fresh by the river. The summer had been hot again, though not so scorching as the year before, and the day the children had arrived the weather had broken, bringing a lot of heavy rain. The river was flowing quite fast today, and the water was a tawny yellow colour.

All was calm in the clearing by the wonderful pool. Magnus took a deep breath, bracing himself for the shock of the cold water, and stepped in. The stones on the bottom were slimy and he slipped about, so he moved forwards, deliberately getting out of his depth. Then he began to swim methodically from one side of the pool to the other, counting. He could cross from one bank to the other in thirty-five strokes, which was the same as doing a length at their local pool. He decided to do at least thirty lengths, before getting out. It would be a long time before he had such a marvellous place to swim again.

At first he loved it, lazily sculling up and down, occasionally edging up to the waterfall which, after the rain, was crashing down quite forcefully into the pool, making a churning yellow-brown foam. He would like to have sat underneath it and let the water run over him, as Floss had done last year, but he was nervous of being pushed under, by the force of it. He knew you should treat all running water with respect.

Eventually, he found himself moving more into the centre of the pool. Here, it was absolutely still, so still that insects had gathered in clouds and he saw dragonflies take off silkily from the glittering surface, and disappear towards the shore. But he was getting cold. He realised that swimming here was very different from a heated indoor pool with a hot shower afterwards. He mustn't take any risks. He began to strike out for the bank, where he'd left his clothes.

But he found, suddenly, that he couldn't make headway. He was doing perfect strokes, exactly as before, except that he had to do them much more vigorously, to propel himself forwards. But he was not moving. He could feel water running strongly against his legs, water that felt like a wide, solid leash, knotting itself round him, pulling him under. The deceptive, still centre of the pool had become the centre of some current, active only, perhaps, after torrential rain. Yet this pool always looked so safe, so innocent? *Why on earth had nobody warned him*?

In panic, he flipped over on to his back and kicked hard, trying to get out of the whirlpool that way. But it was worse than before. The minute he turned over and faced the sky the water pulled him down more forcefully. He knew he was losing his strength, and he went right under, swallowing mouthfuls of brackish water. Now he began to struggle, kicking out desperately, not thinking about swimming any more, doing anything to keep himself afloat. But he was going down a second time. Once more and it would be over.

As he began to drown, the faces of the people he most loved passed across his vision: Father

Godless, the children's mother, David Stickley –
and Arthur, 'Mother' Arthur surrounded by her
kittens. Then there was another face, not in his
mind but actually on the river bank, the ancient
care-worn face of an old woman dressed in
widow's black, who stood there motionless, her
thin white hands clasped together as she stared out
across the water.

Magnus cried, 'Help me, somebody, oh *help
me*!' and a voice came to him across the seething
yellow water, 'I am coming, child, I am coming,
little bird.'

He heard nothing more and he saw nothing.
Afterwards, he remembered nothing except that,
as he was going down into the water for the last
time and it was closing over his head with a great
singing noise, he felt himself being wrapped
round by strong arms, wrapped round and lifted
up. And he felt himself being taken slowly across
the pool, leaning backwards, so it seemed, against
the breast of a mother, before being carried out of
the water and laid gently to rest in the sunshine.

He was to dream many times about this escape
from death, but he told no-one about it, ever,
except that, years afterwards, he tried to describe
what had happened in a letter to Father Godless,
telling him also about the service in the church,
the service for the little boy whose skeleton he had
found, who had at last been laid to rest, and how
that boy's mother had saved his life.

And he always remembered what the old man wrote back to him. How strange and unexpected it was, he said, that saying in the Bible, the one which told us that it wasn't courage that cast out fear, it was love.

THE EMPTY FRAME

Afterword

The Empty Frame is my fifth ghost story. (You will find details of the others at the beginning of this book.) As before, having decided to write about ghosts, I wanted to find a basic story with some real 'meat' in it, to start me off. By this I mean that I didn't want to invent a series of spooky happenings out of my own head. I am not very good at that and if a writer isn't convinced by her own story you may be sure that her readers won't be convinced either.

So I looked around for a convincing story with a ghostly theme on which to base my own book and I found one quite near home. The other books had taken me to Ireland, Cheshire, Scotland and London but I discovered the story for *The Empty Frame* on my own doorstep, in nearby Buckinghamshire where I lived before I moved to Oxford and where I was a schoolteacher.

In a little book called *Discovering Ghosts* I read a story called 'The Blotted Copy Book'. This described the ghost of an Elizabethan lady who has frequently been seen walking about in Bisham Abbey, an ancient house on the Thames, near Marlow. This is now a centre for sport and conferences but in the sixteenth century it was the home of the Hoby family and before that it had been, among other things, a home for the Knights Templar.

The bare bones of the story are these: In Tudor times one of Lady Elizabeth Hoby's sons died a mysterious death. He may have been locked up in a room to get on with his lessons, as a punishment, or he may literally have been forgotten. It is possible that somebody murdered him, or killed him accidentally, in a fit of temper. No body was ever discovered at Bisham but the tradition of the dead child persisted and in the 1850s some workmen, pulling up a floor, discovered a collection of Elizabethan school books. These belonged to a William Hoby and they were said to be full of blots! Unfortunately, and as you might expect, these books have long since disappeared.

From this had developed the story of a 'cruel mother', Lady Elizabeth Hoby, and the idea that she might have driven her son too hard over his lessons, that he was perhaps rather stupid, that possibly she beat him about the head until he died. While it is hard to believe that a mother would have done such a thing (and one theory is that she went riding one day, with young Queen Elizabeth, thinking he was in the care of a servant, and stayed the night at Windsor) it is her ghost that haunts the Abbey and it is certainly very troubled. Tragic Lady Hoby has been seen walking the corridors washing her son's blood from her hands in a basin which floats mysteriously before her. She reminds us of Shakespeare's Lady Macbeth who could not escape from the guilt of killing King Duncan. 'Here's the smell of the blood still; all the perfumes of Arabia will not sweeten this little hand.'

I went to Bisham Abbey to see it for myself and to talk to some of the people who lived and worked there. On arrival I was given a glossy brochure advertising the sports and conference centre. The cover portrayed a ghostly Elizabethan lady (somebody posing for the part of course) walking under an arched doorway. So whatever the truth of the story, the legend had certainly persisted. I learned that at one time school parties had come to stay at Bisham Abbey, to enjoy its sporting facilities, and that some of the children had not liked their quarters very much, particularly those sleeping in the old parts of the Abbey. They reported a strange atmosphere which frightened them. And it was not only young people who had picked up these mysterious feelings. One or two of the sports coaches had also sensed an unhappiness in the air, a sensation that all was not well. I was told that one of them had left altogether and taken a job elsewhere. Of course these are only stories and they may well have been elaborated in the telling, but for the purposes of writing a ghost novel they were excellent material.

After wandering about the Abbey and its

grounds and looking long and hard at the portrait of the formidable and unsmiling Lady Hoby which hangs in its great hall, I made an unforgettable visit to the lady I call 'Miss Adeline' in my story. She knew the Abbey intimately and while she admitted that she herself (like me) had never seen a ghost, and certainly not Lady Hoby, she had heard too much from too many sensible people to dismiss as ridiculous that ghostly sightings of an obviously troubled woman in Elizabethan dress. It was she who told me that the portrait 'did not like to be moved', of how a locked conference room had once had its pretty flower arrangements (daffodils) wrecked, by an unseen hand and how, when the ghost walks in the Abbey, the frame holding the portrait is supposed to turn blank. She told me too of the wounded soldiers who convalesced there in the Second World War and of the nurse who, changing a poultice, heard an inexplicable weeping in the night. Lastly she showed me a scrap of beautiful fabric which may have belonged to Elizabeth the First, who was a frequent visitor when she was young.

From Miss Adeline, I went to Henley Library where I read a history of Bisham Abbey for myself because the author, Piers Compton, had also talked with her. Here I found the story of the retired admiral who, sitting alone in a panelled room after a late game of chess, and 'overlooked by the painting', saw 'Dame Hoby' standing beside him, and fled in terror.

I went home, opened a 'plotting' notebook and sat thinking for a very long time about all I had heard and seen, my brain full of the most marvellous bits and pieces. I knew that I had enough, and more than enough, for my story. But how was I to begin?

Into my head came Magnus, a modern boy who, like William Hoby, had been abused and who had suffered cruelty. In my story his father and mother were both sick in their minds, otherwise he would not have suffered so. But why, I asked myself, did Lady Hoby kill her child? Was she too mentally sick? Or was it an accident? Or did she simply lose her temper and hit him too hard or did she have a tyrannical husband ambitious to succeed at court? Was the death his doing? Could he not tolerate the idea of a stupid son?

Magnus was followed by Floss, desperate to land the part of Lady Macbeth in her school play – a great opportunity for me to explore the theme of guilt. Then practical, no-nonsense Sam came along, Sam who is always on the lookout for scientific explanations for everything but who is at last taken by surprise when he sees Lady Neale for himself.

When I read books for my own enjoyment I greatly dislike it when the plot is neatly tied up at the end, and absolutely everything is 'explained'.

'To see through all things is the same as not to see' said C S Lewis, and I agree with him.

The Empty Frame is meant to keep you guessing. You will never know the real truth behind the story of the dead boy because, in real life, nobody did know. So the book ends with a question mark. The other thing I dislike in my books is an ending of unrelieved sadness and gloom. There is certainly a lot of suffering in *The Empty Frame* but at the end of the story the important things have been resolved and we go forward in hope. William and Magnus hold hands, if you like, across the centuries. The modern boy has laid the Elizabethan boy to rest and his poor tortured mother can have peace at last.

In an act of thanksgiving Lady Neale saves Magnus from death by drowning. Ghosts, as the three children discover, are 'about time' and in the ghost's final action the time barriers are truly crossed. 'Many waters cannot quench love neither can the floods drown it' wrote King Solomon. The story of *The Empty Frame* tells us that love is the strongest force in the world, and that it is indestructible.

Ann Pilling, 1997